"I don't think I've ever seen a woman get herself into as much trouble in as little time. And I always seem to be the cause," Stephen said.

"Just so I know . . . are you planning on getting me into any more trouble, Mr. Gage?"

The flash of intrigue in Stephen's eyes was breathtaking. "Maybe . . . I hope so."

Warmth crept up Lise's neck. The air was so thick with anticipation, she could breathe it. And him. She was breathing him. A low wave of sensation caught her, weakening her legs as if she were standing thigh deep in water.

Stephen saved the moment by rubbing at some paste on her chin with his thumb. "Come on, let me clean you up." He pulled her over to the birdbath and dipped his fingers into the water. Then he tilted her chin upward with one hand and scrubbed gently. Lise was surprised at how easily she surrendered her independence to his wishes.

"Do you like doing this?" she asked. "Babysitting grown women? Taking care of them?"

He smiled. "I like taking care of you." He was scraping softly near her upper lip. "I think I'd like doing anything to you."

A direct hit, Lise thought. The man had good aim. She closed her eyes as he brushed his thumb over her lips. Several soft strokes. *He's not rubbing off paste anymore,* she realized. *He's touching me. Caressing . . . me.*

I ought to stop him, she thought. *But I don't think I can. I like it too much. I like what he does to me.* She wasn't the only one who didn't know if she could stop. . . .

WHAT ARE *LOVESWEPT* ROMANCES?

They are stories of true romance and touching emotion. We believe those two very important ingredients are constants in our highly sensual and very believable stories in the *LOVESWEPT* line. Our goal is to give you, the reader, stories of consistently high quality that may sometimes make you laugh, sometimes make you cry, but are always fresh and creative and contain many delightful surprises within their pages.

Most romance fans read an enormous number of books. Those they truly love, they keep. Others may be traded with friends and soon forgotten. We hope that each *LOVESWEPT* romance will be a treasure—a "keeper." We will always try to publish

LOVE STORIES YOU'LL NEVER FORGET
BY AUTHORS YOU'LL ALWAYS REMEMBER

The Editors

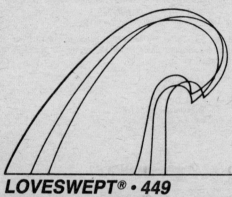

LOVESWEPT® • 449

Suzanne Forster
Lord of Lightning

BANTAM BOOKS
NEW YORK • TORONTO • LONDON • SYDNEY • AUCKLAND

LORD OF LIGHTNING

A Bantam Book / January 1991

LOVESWEPT® *and the wave device are registered*
trademarks of Bantam Books, a division of
Bantam Doubleday Dell Publishing Group, Inc.
Registered in U.S. Patent
and Trademark Office and elsewhere.

If you would be interested in receiving protective vinyl
covers for your Loveswept books, please write to this
address for information:

> *Loveswept*
> *Bantam Books*
> *P. O. Box 985*
> *Hicksville, NY 11802*

ISBN 0-553-44087-X

Published simultaneously in the United States and Canada

Bantam Books are published by Bantam Books, a division
of Bantam Doubleday Dell Publishing Group, Inc. Its trade-
mark, consisting of the words "Bantam Books" and the
portrayal of a rooster, is Registered in U.S. Patent and
Trademark Office and in other countries. Marca Regis-
trada. Bantam Books, 666 Fifth Avenue, New York, New
York 10103.

PRINTED IN THE UNITED STATES OF AMERICA

OPM   0 9 8 7 6 5 4 3 2 1

Lord of Lightning

Prologue

The children saw it first.

The iridescent green cloud hung in the evening sky like an ocean mist, clinging to the darkening foothills of the San Bernardino Mountains. It glowed oddly, almost transparent for several seconds. And then its color deepened to a rich emerald flame against the twilight horizon.

The two youngsters stood side by side, transfixed.

"What is it, Danny?" the girl asked her older brother. She brushed dark bangs from her serious gray eyes and pressed closer to the much-larger boy, tugging on his shirt sleeve. The gravity in her expression contradicted her waiflike appearance. She was slight to the point of spindliness, and looked to be little more than a grade-schooler. "What is it?"

"I don't know, Em," Danny said, hushed. "It looks as if it's coming from the rock quarry."

Set back into the foothills, the quarry was nearly a quarter mile away. It was partially visible through a clearing of thickly wooded sycamores, and as the children began a cautious approach, they noticed a log cabin tucked back into the trees. A windowpane was broken, and the weathered old building appeared to be deserted.

The girl hung back a moment as the boy picked his

way through the undergrowth toward the cabin. "Oh, Danny, look at this!" she cried.

She dropped to a crouch near the limp form of a sparrow hawk, its graceful head wrenched backward as through its neck had been broken.

"Don't touch it, Em," Danny called out to her as she bent to scoop the bird up. "It's dead. There's nothing you can do."

"But it's so beautiful—"

"Emily!"

Danny's voice had a frantic sound. As Emily looked up he was sprinting toward her, waving her away from the bird.

"What is it?" she said.

"I heard something in the bushes behind the cabin." He caught hold of her hand and pulled her to her feet, dragging her with him toward the cover of the nearby sycamores. "Come on, Em. Something's out there!"

Emily's breath burned through her nose as they huddled behind a thicket of mountain laurel and manzanita, their eyes fixed on the cabin. "What do you think it is?"

The answer constricted in Danny's throat.

A silvery flash of light appeared in the wooded darkness across the way, and he jerked Em close as if to silence an imminent scream. Immobile as graveyard statuary, the two children watched the silvery flashes draw nearer, taking on substance and form.

The luminescent being that emerged from the side of the cabin moved like a man, a very large man, encased in a shimmering metallic skin from head to toe. His features were hidden from view by the dark glow of a face shield, and the apparatus he carried looked ominously like a space-age weapon.

Em and Danny ducked down as the man scanned the area thoroughly, saw the bird, and walked to it. He knelt down and murmured something, then he picked up the limp form and touched its head. The bird twitched and went still again.

Silver flashed in the waning light as the man stood. Suddenly the bird fluttered in the cupped hands, and a weak cry burst from its broken body. In the next moment the creature was all flying wings and graceful, harrowing energy. Silhouetted by an iridescent green aura, it soared into the falling night, its cries echoing sweetly in the foothills.

One

Had Lise Anderson foreseen the fateful consequences
of roaming the Tools 'R Us Hardware Store with a
gimpy shopping cart that bright June afternoon, she
might have decided to trade the conveyance in for a
smoother running model. She might even have decided
to shop on another day. At another hardware store.

But Lise wasn't thinking about consequences as she
browsed in the electronics section, mulling over step-
down transformers and rheostats, just two of the high-
tech gizmos she needed for her class's science project
the next day. She was wondering how in the world
she was going to teach twenty rambunctious summer
school students to build a model metrorail when she
had trouble telling a monkey wrench from a pair of
duckbill pliers.

" 'Connect the red wire to the blue terminal at junc-
tion A,' " she mumbled, reading the transformer
instructions to herself as she muscled her wayward
shopping cart down the aisle. A pyramid of oil cans
loomed to her left. She saw it out of the corner of her
eye and made an automatic adjustment for it as she
continued reading. " 'Make sure the local electric
power is AC. If the wires touch adjacent terminals, a
severe shock can result.' "

That was when her shopping cart escaped from her.

With a will of its own the cart locked into a curve,

4

wheels jamming, ball bearings screeching. Lise threw her body weight behind it, trying to right the stubborn thing with one hand while she clutched the transformer with the other.

"Swell," she muttered, unsurprised. She was a battle-scarred veteran of the renegade shopping cart syndrome. Her particular peeve was with carts that headed straight for parked cars in the store lots, as though they were designed to search out and destroy.

She twisted, heaved, and swore under her breath, but none of her gyrations made any difference. The cart lurched like a demon possessed for the oil cans.

One last urgent yank brought the cart around. Wheels screeched, axles ground, and Lise heaved a sigh of relief. As she squeaked past the pyramid and rolled into the plumbing section, she glanced behind her. Home free. Not even one can of thirty-weight motor oil had tumbled to the floor.

She never saw the other shopping cart approaching. Or its operator.

"Oh, no!" The transformer slipped from her hand as the two carts collided head on, and a shower of electronic minutia bounced out of Lise's upper tray. Throw switches, battery sleeves, switch brackets, and connectors flew every which way, scattering like a string of pearls.

"I'm *sorry*," Lise cried as the dropped into a crouch and began scooping up debris. "My shopping cart—"

"Right," he said, laughing softly. "The shopping cart from hell. Mine too."

Lise barely registered the low ripple of masculine laughter as she knelt to clean up the mess. She was too busy piling connectors and switch brackets into the crook of her arm. She reached for the transformer just as the man knelt to help her.

Lise saw it coming, another collision, but she was as helpless to stop it as she had been the cart. Her bare arm brushed against his as they touched the metal casing at exactly the same instant. Lise felt as though she'd stuck a wet wire in a live socket. Their hands met and the jolt of electricity that rolled up her arm seemed hot enough to scorch off the fine blond hairs.

What happened next seemed to defy the laws of physics. Lise stared in disbelief as a tiny arc of green lightning connected their fingers. Spiky and white-hot, it was visible even in the harsh glare of the store lights. "Good Lord," she breathed, realizing that the spark couldn't have come from the transformer. It wasn't plugged in!

Seemingly endless seconds flashed by before Lise had the presence of mind to pull her hand away. She had no idea how much time had actually elapsed. The entire incident played like a horror movie scene in slow motion.

In the aftermath of the physical shock, a ringing sensation filled her ears, and the odor that burned in her nostrils smelled faintly of sulfur, as though a match had just been struck.

"What happened?" she asked as the man gripped her arm and helped her to her feet, steadying her as she emptied her load of electronic paraphernalia into the tray.

"I think we shorted out," he said.

"We certainly did." Lise laughed shakily and stepped away from him. "I'm surprised we didn't black out the entire store."

Lise's first impression was of faded blue jeans, a chambray shirt, and a log-splitter's shoulders. An outdoorsman, she thought, registering his dusty gold hair and several days' growth of beard. As their gazes connected Lise felt another kind of lightning. A type of déjà vu—not quite the feeling that she'd met him before, but that she knew him somehow. The sense of recognition was powerful. Its clarity confounded Lise because there was nothing to confirm it. Her mind searched for the details of a meeting, any kind of a memory, but she came up empty-handed. There was no corroborating data, no personal history to be found, not even a glimmer. "Do I know you?" she asked.

He took a slow, contemplative moment to study her.

"I find myself wishing I could say yes. But no, you don't know me. It's impossible."

Impossible . . .

Lise examined him quite openly then, taking in his height—well over six feet—and his husky, blue-collar build. Dark blond hair cascaded carelessly to his shoulders, and the beard that chased his angular jawline was shot through with gold and a darker hue, bronze. A head-turner, she thought. Not handsome detail for detail, but arresting taken as a whole. If infinity had a color, she decided, it would be the blue of his eyes. To describe them as dense didn't begin to do them justice. They looked as though they could absorb all the light in the room.

"I'm sorry," she said finally. "You remind me of someone."

"Who?"

"I don't know . . ." Usually Lise wasn't one to equivocate, even when she was off balance, which she very definitely was at the moment. But she couldn't shake the confusion, or the certainty that he was someone she'd met, perhaps even a shaping influence in her past.

And then it came to her. Of course, she thought, smiling to herself as she remembered the stories her Scandinavian mother used to entertain her with on rainy afternoons. Legends about flaxen-haired beauties, about seafaring Vikings and Norse gods. Odin, Heimdall, and Thor—men like golden lions.

As a child she'd spent endless hours imagining herself being carried off by some enthralling Viking warlord, sailing through stormy seas on his long ship. That was where she knew this man from, she realized, her childhood fantasies, the pages of ancient mythology. Slightly disconcerted, she brushed stray hairs back from her face, and felt the flush of warmth in her cheeks.

"Are you new here in Shady Tree?" she asked, aware that the store's customers were making a wide and curious path around them. Of course he was, she thought. There were exactly two thousand and three residents in Shady Tree according to the latest census. Soon to be two thousand five with Peggy Latimer expecting twins. Lise knew every one of the city's proud sons and daughters, and this fellow, with his Viking bones and hair the color of winter sunshine, wasn't one of them.

He scooped up the transformer and handed it to her. "I'm on vacation. A geologist. Some people call us rock hounds."

"I'm Lise Anderson," she said. "The grade-school teacher."

"*The* grade-school teacher?"

"Well, Harlan Meek usually teaches math and science, but he's on sabbatical this summer, so I'm the only show in town."

Lise felt another mild shock as she took the transformer from him. Only this time it was rather a pleasant sensation. A tingly warmth spread up her arm, and her fingertips went slightly numb. "Did you feel that too?" she asked.

He smiled unexpectedly and it did such intriguing things to his face, Lise found herself smiling back. Quite a silly smile, she imagined. If she'd ever stared at a man the way she was staring at him, she couldn't remember when.

"We seem to have our wires crossed," he said.

It was an offhand reference, a throwaway line, Lise realized, but the undertones were sexy. Even his voice was a little grainy, and the sound of it gave her an unexpected thrill. Nerves sparkled, and a depth charge headed for the reaches of her stomach. When a man's tone went husky like that, it put a woman in mind of one thing and one thing only. Sex.

"One of us had better be grounded the next time we touch," she said. "Or the results could be fatal."

His eyes lit with laughter. "Not a bad way to go. Must be the dry weather."

"I don't think weather has anything to do with it," Lise responded softly.

He stared at her oddly, and Lise wondered if she was being too straightforward again. She knew the folks around Shady Tree said that Lise Anderson, gentle-mannered, understated beauty though she was, was a little too plainspoken for her own good. She'd scared off all the eligible men with her honesty, they said. Lise had heard the rumors.

He rolled his cart back and took the only item from it, a small white carton, as though he meant to leave. "You didn't ask, but my name is Stephen Gage," he said, tucking the box under his arm. "I'm staying in the Cooper cabin outside of town."

"The Cooper place? You're really isolated out there."

He shrugged. "I'm used to being alone. Besides, your local mountains are supposed to have some rare min-eral deposits. I wanted to check them out."

"Will you be around long?" Lise could hardly believe she was grilling him this way. She rarely—make that *never*—came onto men. She hadn't even dated in years. At twenty-seven, people were already beginning to call her a spinster, and oddly enough, she didn't mind. She'd never felt the need of a man underfoot. But this man was so oddly compelling with his winter smile and his electric touch, the thought of not seeing him again gave her a pang.

"No, not long." He inclined his head slightly as though he'd read her mind. "But I have the feeling you and I are going to run into each other again."

"Yes . . . so do I."

Lise heard a soft beeping sound, and thought for one crazy moment that it was her own heartbeat. She looked around the store for a smoke alarm or a security device, and then she noticed the small black case attached to his belt. "I think your beeper's going off," she said.

"Beeper? What's that?"

She thought he must be kidding, but he looked so totally blank, so devoid of any comprehension of the word, she quickly pointed to the case.

He unhooked the device, smiled at her, and slipped it into his back pocket. "Thanks," was all he said.

They were both silent a moment, regarding each other, the situation suddenly full of promise and possibility. Lise kept thinking she ought to say something, but she had no idea what it would be. Backlit by neon, his hair was afire with silver light, like sun breaking through the rain. Lise was struck by it. She almost mentioned it, and then he saved her from the certain embarrassment. He acknowledged her with his eyes, and a barely discernible nod, and then he swung around and disappeared down the aisle.

Lise was left to stare after him, softened and bemused. Now what was that all about, she thought. As she turned to the errant shopping cart she glanced at her watch. It took her a moment to realize that the second hand wasn't moving. Her watch had stopped! Without knowing how she knew, she realized it had happened at exactly the moment he'd touched her.

"He's got a *primo* ray gun! I saw it. And he can make dead birds fly!"

"Yeah! My big brother says he's an extraterrestrial."

"An extra what?"

The children's excited voices flew through the open classroom window of Abraham Lincoln Grade School, distracting Lise as she laid out the various items for the model railroad turnpike they would be starting that morning. She listened to the chatter a moment and smiled. Last week it was *Nintendo*. This week it was ray guns and spacemen. The kids were always revved up about something. There must have been a science fiction movie on TV over the weekend.

"An extraterrestrial, barf breath!" one of the boys snorted indignantly. "Like E.T., only bigger."

"Yeah, butt face," another boy chimed in, "a man from Mars!"

Lise clicked her tongue. Later she planned to have a word with those two young men about their language. It was going to be a challenging day, she could tell. The first day of model construction. The state science fair was imminent, and her students had chosen a project beyond their abilities, she feared. Certainly beyond hers. She'd agreed because building the model metrorail would be a wonderful learning experience, and she also hoped it would make a favorable impression on the county school board.

Lately the board had been making noises about converting the grade school into a community center and bussing the kids to Redlands, where, they contended, the students would get a better education in a more modern facility. Lise wanted to show them that Lincoln's students were top-notch and weren't being deprived. And what better way, she'd decided, than by winning a statewide science fair?

"Miss Anderson, did you hear about the UFO?" The class suddenly turned its attention to her.

"We're being invaded, Miss Anderson, by a whole fleet of puke-green flying saucers! They landed in the rock quarry!"

Lise nodded patiently. "What have you kids been up to? Reading those dreadful science fiction comics again?"

A chorus rang out. "It wasn't a comic book! It really happened!"

Each of their versions of that weekend's excitement was more fantastic than the next. From what Lise could determine, someone had noticed strange lights in the foothills, and although no one had actually seen the UFO, Danny Baxter claimed to have been an eyewitness to some startling occurrences. He'd seen an alien life-form, he said, a huge silver creature who packed a ray gun.

With a little more probing, Lise determined that Danny was the only actual witness. And because she knew a little about his background, she couldn't help but wonder if he might be making the whole thing up. The ten-year-old was from a broken home, and he'd reacted to the upheaval in his life by becoming boisterous and demanding the attention his beleaguered mother wasn't always able to give him.

"Danny," Lise said gently, "I know it's fun to kid around with your friends, but you could frighten people with a story like that."

"I'm not lying," Danny said, desperation in his voice. "I really saw him, I swear."

"I saw him, too, Miss Anderson. I saw the spaceman."

The quiet declaration came from Emily Baxter, Danny's younger sister. Lise turned to see the five-year-old standing in the doorway. One look at Emily's clasped hands and her pensive gray eyes and Lise lost her heart all over again. It had gotten so she couldn't lay eyes on the somber little girl without wanting to smooth her hair and comfort her. Emily's reaction to their family's breakup had been much different than Danny's. She had withdrawn into watchful silences, observing the world through wide, sad eyes as though passing sentence on its casual cruelties. She was a five-year-old going on thirty-something.

Lise remembered vividly how Em had wandered off the year before and gotten lost in a spring rainstorm. The whole town had mobilized for the search, but Lise had been the one to find Em trudging doggedly through the foothills. The child had told Lise she was following the rainbow to its treasure. "When I find it, my mom won't have to work so hard," she'd said. Lise had been touched by the child's concern, and then she'd looked up at the sky, smiling through a sparkle of tears as she remembered how magical rainbows had been for her as a child. Perhaps that was the beginning of the special bond between her and Em.

Now, Lise approached the child and knelt beside her, taking her hand. "What did you see, Emily?"

"I saw a man pick up a dead bird, and then it flew away."

"What did the man look like?"

"Just like Danny said. He was big and silver all over."

"Hey, Teach!" Julie Watson's helmeted head popped into the doorway behind Emily. "You talking about our visitor from Mongo? I heard he was ten feet tall with X-ray eyes and a particle weapon gun."

"*Wow*," Danny breathed. "Is that what it was?"

"A particle weapon gun!" another voice squeaked.

The children began to chatter again. Lise squeezed Emily's hand reassuringly and released it.

"Julie," Lise said, "please, don't encourage them."

Lanky and quick, Julie pulled off her motorcycle helmet, shook her long auburn hair free, and swung into the room. She was Lise's teaching assistant on her summer break from college, and at nineteen she hadn't yet outgrown her tomboy ways. She was wonderful with the children though, and Lise found her help invaluable.

"It's all over town," Julie continued, tossing her helmet onto a nearby desk. "He's holed up in the old Cooper place. Some of the guys from Frank's Gas Station are getting a welcoming party together. They're going to check him out."

Lise stood. "The Cooper place?"

Julie nodded, and Lise laughed in surprise. "I know that man," she said. "I ran into him in the hardware store yesterday. He's not an alien. He's a geologist. On vacation."

"What's a geologist?" someone whispered.

"I think it's like a Romulan on *Star Trek*," a voice whispered back.

Julie looked skeptical. "The hardware store? Maybe he was getting batteries for his particle ray gun."

Julie was a science fiction movie buff, and Lise knew her assistant would just love to wring every drop of drama out of the "visitation" scenario. As much as she hated to ruin the fun, Lise was concerned about Julie's reference to a welcoming party.

"I certainly hope those rowdies at Frank's don't go out to the Cooper place and stir up trouble," she said. "Why, Stephen Gage is a perfectly nice man. He'll think we're a bunch of yokels."

Lise walked to the classroom window and glanced down the street in the direction of the gas station. All looked calm, but she was still uneasy about the town's reaction to their visitor. "Maybe I should run out there myself and officially welcome Mr. Gage to Shady Tree. That would put a stop to the rumors. Really," she murmured, still staring out the window, "he's perfectly harmless."

Well, maybe not harmless, she thought, correcting herself. The man packed enough voltage to stop a charging bull. Remembering the shopping cart collision, the odd physical sensations, and her own completely uncharacteristic reactions, she brought a hand to the lapel of her shirtwaist dress. Her fingers worked absently as she stared out the window. A moment later she stopped short and glanced down, realizing she'd unbuttoned her own dress. She did it back up again, and when she turned around, Julie and most of her students were gazing at her intently.

"What is it?" Lise asked.

Julie posed the question rather archly. "What does this Stephen Gage guy look like?"

Lise shrugged. "He's . . . average." Right, she thought, just your average Viking warrior-chieftain. She glanced around the room at twenty pairs of bright, curious eyes and realized she was smiling.

"Average meaning brown hair, brown suit, and brown shoes?"

"No, Julie," Lise said, just a hint of sarcasm in her tone. "Average meaning six feet two, plus or minus an inch, drop-dead blond hair and blue eyes."

Julie grinned. "When's the wedding?"

Lise knew she was foolish to let the conversation go on even a minute longer. Forty little ears were listening, and the town was already interested enough in her unpromising love life.

"There is a lesson in this for all of us, I think," she said, addressing the children. "We must never judge people by their appearance. And certainly not by rumors and innuendo. Mr. Gage is a visitor to our town, and therefore, every courtesy should be extended to him."

"So let me get this straight," Julie persisted. "You're actually thinking about going out to the Cooper place tonight and welcoming this person to Shady Tree? After everything you've heard here today? One skinny woman against a six-foot alien with a death ray?"

Lise gave Julie a sharp warning glance. "Someone has to put a stop to these silly rumors. Besides, I think I may have picked up something of his by mistake at the hardware store." That was true enough, she thought, extending her authority to the children with a silencing tilt of her head. There'd been an unexplained package of copper wiring among her things when she checked out at the register.

The class went quiet. Julie tapped her chin thoughtfully.

"I still don't think you should go alone," Julie said after a moment, then grinned irrepressibly. "But whatever you do, don't let him hold your hand. That's how the alien in *Barbarella* made love."

Two

Lise Anderson was immobilized. And very impatient with herself because of it. Heaving a sigh, she stared out the front windshield of her secondhand Cordoba, still in cream puff condition except for a patch of oxidizing maroon paint and a loose hood ornament, and wondered why she was sitting in the driveway of her house. She'd been there, contemplating the horizon, for at least a half an hour. Perhaps longer, she thought. The sun was starting to set, and soon it would be dark.

This is childish, Lise, she told herself. If she wanted to go out there and welcome the man to Shady Tree, why didn't she just do it? The package of copper wiring sat on the car seat beside her, all the excuse she needed. There was also the necessity of stopping the escalating gossip, a very real problem in a small, rural community. Shady Tree wasn't Los Angeles. It wasn't even San Bernardino. The residents were close-knit, protective, and quickly roused to action when they perceived a threat. Yes, she ought to go. It was the appropriate thing to do.

A half hour later she was pulling off the arterial highway onto a smaller road that branched into the foothills. In the distance, carbon-black mountains seduced a flaming red sun into their hoary depths. Struck by the beauty, Lisa cracked the car window to let in cooling air, fragrant with pine and sage.

She loved the sinuous landscape of the hills, the rolling, sage-kissed chaparral, the black oak and juniper trees. Whenever her schedule allowed, she escaped to the hill country, to walk, to pick wildflowers, and to be alone. Even though she would miss her students terribly, she often thought she would make a very good hermit. Her spirit seemed to require the renewal of solitude. Her senses preferred simplicity.

There were drawbacks to her self-imposed isolation, however. Occasionally she paid a heavy price in loneliness. It didn't happen often, but there were evenings when she longed for someone to share her innermost thoughts with. Some wishes had to be told to come true. Some dreams needed a coconspirator.

But that kind of intimacy also had its price.

The road branched off again, a rutted dirt access way that tested the Cordoba's shocks with every jolt. Lisa took the bumps stoically. Like the car, she wore her scars well. She'd long ago decided that independence was too precious a commodity to risk in the marketplace of human relationships. At eighteen, she'd fought a long and bitter battle with her father for autonomy, for self-rule. The victory had been sweet, but it had cost her his love. And it had torn away a piece of her heart . . .

A flash of crimson light pulled Lise out of her reverie. It was the sun's last gasp, and she was grateful for its timing.

The deserted cabin was nestled back in the trees. Lise spotted it as she drove into the clearing, only it didn't look deserted. There was a light glowing dimly through the window, and the broken pane had been replaced.

She parked the Cordoba and let herself out, glancing around for any sign of the strange phenomena the children had described. The forested landscape looked normal for that time of the evening. Warm carmine light glowed through the darkening woods, and the rock quarry, though some distance away, was partially visible through the trees.

It was just as Lise had thought. The children had seen something out here, perhaps Stephen Gage ministering to a wounded bird, but their imaginations had taken over from there. Relief washed over her, bringing with it the realization that she *had* been nervous. She would give Mr. Gage his copper wire, warn him of the rumors, and have a good laugh about them. Then she would leave.

No one answered her knock. Lise tested the door and found it locked and bolted. A glance in the window convinced her that no one was inside. One lamp glowed in the corner of a sparsely furnished living area, illuminating the uninhabited room.

The tightness in her chest was disappointment, she realized. She had wanted to see him again, even just a glimpse, to see if he would have the same crazy effect on her nervous system. She was more than a little curious about the electric shocks, and she remembered vividly that odd, grasping sensation deep in her stomach. Staring at the package in her hand, she considered leaving it on his doorstep. Instead, she carried it with her back to the Cordoba.

The car radio blared on as she keyed the ignition. The static was deafening, and as she reached to switch the radio off, she saw something that astonished her. A greenish vapor was seeping from the rock quarry. Faintly iridescent, it drifted and plumed like smoke from a huge bonfire. Lise switched off the ignition, her fingers curling around the keys. A pulse beat near her thumb where the metal ridge pressed into her flesh. *What in the world?* A forest fire just starting?

She got out of the car, at war with her instincts, which told her not to go one step farther. They also told her quite emphatically to get the heck out of there, to find someone who could help her check it out. Preferably someone large and powerful. Nevertheless, she started for the overgrown path that led to the quarry. Just to get a closer look, she told herself. The weather had been extremely dry recently, and there'd been a rash of summer lightning storms. If it was a fire, she should notify the authorities immediately.

The quarry was surrounded by a rocky border a dozen feet high and raised like the cone of a small volcano, which made it impossible for Lise to see the interior from her vantage point on the path. It looked uncannily like a moon crater, she thought, names flashing through her mind as she remembered a science class she'd taught for Harlan Meek . . . the Apennines, the lunar Alps and the great Carpathians, all mountains of the moon.

The mist began to look more like light than vapor as she neared. It took on luminous tones as the sky darkened, shimmering and dancing, the green deepening to emerald before it fanned out in plumes. A faint smell of ether hung in the air.

By this time Lise's curiosity had all but silenced the warning messages in her head. She wasn't going to be able to stop until she'd seen for herself what was going on. Accepting that fact, she proceeded cautiously, but steadily, toward the quarry.

Gravel crunched beneath the soles of her leather sandals as the path fanned out into glacial streams of rock that cascaded from the quarry walls. She'd changed from her high heels, but she was still wearing the shirtwaist dress she'd chosen for school that day. Now she wished she'd worn something more suitable, and warmer.

The night sky was darkening rapidly as Lise began to climb the gradual rise. The rocks gave way under her weight, making her ascent as laborious as trudging in sand. Sharp pebbles worked their way into her sandals, forcing her to stop and shake them out. She was digging a fragment from the ball of her foot when she heard the sound. Crackling like static on a telephone line, it came from the quarry.

Lise was practically on all fours by the time she reached the crest and looked into the quarry. What she saw there made her drop to her knees in astonishment. The basin of the craterlike form was ablaze with a brilliant blue-green fire.

The brightness forced her to shield her eyes. It was staggering to look at—a turquoise inferno—but without heat. Only that incessant buzzing sound. Or was it a clicking? She couldn't take it all in.

A darkness moved behind the sheets of flaming light. Lise pushed to her feet, trying to make out the apparitional form. It flowed like mercury, taking different shapes. Her heart was beating wildly, but curiosity held her in place. Was it an illusion? A shadow? She inched down the steep grade for a closer look and stopped abruptly as the vaporous form seemed to float in her direction. It might have been the body shape of a man, she realized, only it looked larger, much larger.

The gravel gave way beneath Lise, and by the time she'd stopped her slide, she realized she'd entered the aura. The light drew in around her, gauzy and surreal, eddying like an azure tide. The color intensified, and she felt a prickling sensation run along her skin, rifling the hair on her arms. An ethereal odor filled her nostrils, burning the tender membranes.

Lise lurched backward. If the light was actually some sort of gaseous substance, it could be poisonous. She'd heard of things like marsh gas, but never in the mountains. Panic caught her as she floundered in the rock bed. The gravel sank beneath her with the deadly suction of quicksand as she wrenched around and fought for traction. Digging in, propelling herself upward, she burst into the fresh air. *Air.* It seared into her lungs in several sharp gasps.

She was halfway up the cone when she heard a hiss of sound and glanced back. The darkness was a black wraith swimming in blue fire. It grew larger and more distinct by the second. Lise could discern a domelike head and appendages that might have been arms. That's when she realized it was moving closer. *It was following her.*

Adrenaline burst through her body. She heaved herself toward the crest of the cone, laboring frantically to reach it. A stitch of pain caught her as she reached the top, and the sharpness doubled her over as if she were a stricken marathoner. She clutched her side and dropped to one knee, fighting to get up again. Through the trees, she could see the clearing where her car was parked. *Just let me get there*, she thought.

She started down the slope, pitching forward as her foot snagged something. An instant later she was tumbling helplessly down the rocky decline.

Even if Lise had seen the boulder that lay in her path, she wouldn't have had the strength or the control to avoid it. The blow caught her in the ribs and solar plexus, knocking the wind out of her, a collision of flesh and bone against solid granite.

The last thing she saw before she lost consciousness was an amorphous silvery form descending upon her.

Hushed by night's descent, the foothills became a moonlit temple, sanctuary to a thousand nocturnal creatures. A coyote howled in the distance, the sound forlorn. As the cry faded a sparrow hawk swooped through the clearing and landed on the front porch railing of the Cooper cabin. Silvery-winged in the moonlight, it seemed to be standing guard, a vigilant sentry.

Inside the cabin Stephen Gage was contemplating the unconscious woman he'd just settled on his bed. He'd checked her for breaks at the quarry and had found only lacerations and bruises. Her breathing was normal, and there were no apparent concussions, but some of the cuts looked deep. They would have to be treated to prevent infection.

A flash of silver caught his eye as he turned. Seeing his own reflection in the dresser mirror, he realized he hadn't changed out of his protective gear. He unzipped the disposable suit at the shoulders first, pulling off the gloved sleeves as though they were pieces of a sewing pattern.

A moment later the rest of the jumpsuit lay pooled around his feet. He stepped out of it, swept up the cellophane-thin, antistatic material and walked to the cabin's enclosed back porch to discard it in a sealed metal container.

When he returned to the room moments later with an antiseptic solution and some bandages to dress her wounds, she had shifted to her side and thrown her hand above her head. The position made her look fragile and feminine, even faintly tragic. He stopped to study her, struck by the vulnerability she'd unknowingly exposed to his eyes. It hit him then that she *was* vulnerable. A woman unconscious on a strange man's bed.

She was beautiful, he realized, surprised that he hadn't noticed it before, in the store. He'd found her attractive then, but now, in repose, he could see the simplicity inherent in her bone structure and the brushed golden tones in her skin. The sunny streaks in her wheat-colored hair highlighted the plaits of her French braid, which was coiled and pinned at her nape. He remembered her eyes. They were a strange pale blue, like dawn on a cloudy day. Beautiful eyes, he decided. She was a woman who brought fundamental things to mind—dawn, sunshine, the elements.

He sat down on the bed next to her, and with a dampened cloth, began to clean the cut on her forehead. She stirred, but didn't wake. When she did, he knew he would have to find a way to quickly reassure her that she was safe. He didn't want her panicking again. She'd already done herself enough damage.

He cleaned the cuts on her arm, and then attempted to roll her to her back so that he could clean the arm she was lying on. She moaned softly as he lifted and repositioned her. That was when he saw the rip in her dress and the gash that began at her rib cage and ran alongside her breast to her armpit. Though she was no longer bleeding, there were some violent looking bruises. It was possible she'd broken some ribs.

He rose slowly, staring at her, his heart thudding.

He was going to have to undress her to get to the wound.

The brutal irony of it hit him immediately. Undressing a beautiful woman would have been a fantasy come true for most men—but Stephen Gage wasn't most men. And he had no intention of subjecting himself to that kind of cruel and unusual punishment. It would be ludicrous to think that he could treat her wounds with any kind of clinical detachment. She was injured, but that wasn't nearly as significant to him as the fact that she was an injured *woman*.

It had been a long time since he'd touched a woman in any condition. Until recently, it had been years since he'd *seen* a woman, and he wasn't willing to put himself to the test of seeing one naked—or of undressing her himself. Not yet. And not her, he thought. She was too desirable, a mantrap lying in wait, an ambush rigged with irresistible female secrets. And she was helpless to defend herself against a man dangerously low on self-control.

His moral dilemma quickly became irrelevant. He couldn't call an ambulance. It would draw attention to the quarry lights, and to himself—a risk he wasn't willing to take. He also couldn't let her lay there and bleed. If her ribs were broken, they would have to be wrapped. He considered waking her, and decided it would be easier for both of them if she remained out cold. He wouldn't have to deal with her resistance and/ or embarrassment. She wouldn't have to watch him sweat it out, trying to appear indifferent.

Her lightweight cotton dress buttoned down the front, and Stephen could see immediately that he had two choices. Remove the dress totally, or take half-measures. He could draw the top down and let it bunch around her waist.

The dress had to go, he decided. The bunched material would hamper him. He sat next to her, aware that there was only one place to begin, the buttons at her neckline. His eyes were drawn to the rise and fall of her breasts beneath the peach-colored fabric. They looked full and softly rounded, almost too large for her slender frame. Just his luck, he thought, exhaling tightly, the first woman he'd come near in over three years, and she had to be built.

Humor did nothing to alleviate his tension. He worked open the first button, and his mouth went dry as his fingers accidentally slipped inside the placket of her dress. He hesitated as his skin brushed hers. *Velvet doesn't even come close*, he thought. He'd never felt anything so soft.

He had four more buttons free when he noticed the sprinkling of freckles beneath his fingers. They dusted the valley between her breasts and disappeared into the shadows of her cleavage. Freckles and cleavage, he thought, his heart beginning to thud again. It was a dangerous combination.

He worked open the next few buttons, slowly, awkwardly, until he had the dress undone to her waist. She stirred a little, her breath escaping in a soft sigh as he grazed her skin, and the sound of it made his stomach tighten. It was a whisper as seductive as the hollow sensation inside him. It tugged at him irresistibly.

He stood then, staring down at her, his mind beginning to play tricks on him. It was telling him that perhaps she knew what he was doing, that perhaps she even liked it. A fantasy took shape in his imagination . . . a supine woman, drugged with passion, languidly allowing a man to undress her, waiting for him to take her sweetly, aching for the hardening organ between his legs. *Take me, she whispered, reaching out for him, opening her legs in lush invitation . . .*

A film of sweat dampened Stephen's neck as he broke free of the gripping scenario. He strode to the cabin window and stared out. He was in worse shape than he'd thought. The muscles in his groin ached like fire. He wasn't going to be able to do this, he realized. Even if he could keep his actions under control, he couldn't control his mind. Or his body. He was responding involuntarily, muscles hardening even as he stood across the room, ten feet from her.

It had been too long. He no longer understood the drives and inhibitions of a normal man. He had come from a world where women didn't exist. Where life itself barely existed. He had lost touch with the human race.

A moment later he came face-to-face with the reality of his predicament. He had no choice. He couldn't let anyone else come to the cabin to take care of her. Paramedics roaring around with their vans and flashing lights would be too risky to the vital things he had to accomplish.

He turned back and glanced at her, disgusted at himself. A woman was hurt and he was acting like an adolescent kid with his first girlie magazine. "Get it together, Gage," he muttered.

He got the dress off her fairly quickly once he made up his mind to do it. It wasn't as tortuous as he'd expected, but her soft sighs every time he touched her didn't make the task any easier. He could have sworn she was responding to him, or if not that, then dreaming about something she shouldn't have been. Either way, it was playing hell with his good intentions.

His jaw muscles clenched as he let his eyes brush over her. She wore nothing under the dress but a pair of soft cotton panties and a cotton bra. No slip, no nylons. No lace. Interesting, he thought grimly, the no-frills model. She apparently harbored no secret fantasies if her sensible underwear was any indication.

Unfortunately he had fantasies enough for both of them. He averted his eyes, swearing violently as it flashed through his head again, the wildly sexy scenario . . . only this time *she* was the languid woman, reaching out to him, opening her legs, aching to be taken. . . .

His stomach fisted painfully. Get it over with, *Gage!*

He lifted her, forcing himself to be gentle—and to ignore her murmurous sighs as he ran his hand along the crevice between her shoulder blades. He was feeling for the back closure of her bra, but all he found was warm skin and elastic fabric. Puzzled, he laid her back down and scanned the front of the bra.

There was a small plastic oval at the bottom center of the bra where the cups came together. He tested it gingerly, then slipped his forefinger underneath it and felt the two interlocking sections give way. Ingenious, he thought, applying pressure, a front opening. The bra clicked open, and he smiled, pleased with himself. Mission accomplished.

It didn't hit him for a moment what he'd done. He'd become so engrossed in the mechanics of the brassiere that he hadn't thought about the fact that he was baring her breasts. A nerve twitched in his jaw as he surveyed the results of his handiwork. *Lush* was the word that came to mind. Lord, yes. Her breasts were fuller than he'd imagined, almost voluptuously heavy.

There was only one problem. The long S-shaped gash had caught the underside of her right breast. In order to clean away the encrusted blood, he would have to cup her, lift her— An angry sound hissed through his clenched teeth. *Feeling a woman up.* Wasn't that what they called it?

A moment later he was gingerly cleaning the long gash, and praying to heaven that she wouldn't shift or sigh or do anything else that would push him over the edge. As he worked his way down from her armpit, he cupped her breast with one hand and dabbed at the injury with the other. It was a nasty cut, and he didn't want to hurt her, but that concern did nothing to alleviate the massive fisting in his groin.

Stephen Gage was in pain.

The silky weight of her in his palm was devastating. She was soft beyond belief, and her nipples were slightly budded. From the cold, he hoped. To a man in his extreme state of deprivation, she represented more than a sexual release. At that moment she was everything he'd ever dreamed of in those lost years of ice and eternal darkness.

By the time he'd finished with her, he was sheened in sweat and his breathing was shallow. He actually felt a wave of dizziness wash over him as he covered her with a blanket.

As he rose and stood back he caught his reflection in the mirror across the room. He was a frightening sight, his eyes wild and lonely, his features gaunt. He stared at himself, struck by the raw pain he saw. . . .

The image unlocked a memory. Another time. Another woman. *Another world.* It ripped through his mind, uncoiling like a demon storm, shrieking of tragedy, of darkness and death. It reminded him of what he'd done—of who he was. It warned him that he was an exiled man, forever marked.

"*No,*" he breathed, fisting his hands, driving the memory away with a massive force of will. In its aftermath he could feel the pain coming, but he was powerless to stop it. His strength was gone. It began as it always did, with a blinding flash of white light, and then several crimson flares burned into his focus like laser beams, searing his brain. He caught the web of his hand between his thumb and forefinger, gripping himself brutally, applying enough pressure to snap bones. The man in the mirror was disintegrating before his eyes, dissolving in a pale, fiery light.

In his total concentration he didn't see that Lise's eyes had fluttered open, and she was watching him.

Three

Lise's first semiconscious thought was that she must still be dreaming. Through the misty veil of her half-closed eyes, she saw what appeared to be a great golden lion hovering over her.

She might have screamed if she hadn't felt so drugged and stuporous. Lethargy dragged at her as she tried to move, and a dull pain throbbed near her right breast. The question floating vaguely in her mind was, *Where am I?* The only sound she heard in the utter stillness was the soft rasp of her own breathing.

Her eyes were heavy-lidded and burning with exhaustion. Fighting to stay conscious, she let them droop shut. For several seconds she sank back into dreamy oblivion, drifting in darkness, telling herself she mustn't let go completely. When she forced her eyes open again, the form above her had transformed from a lion to a man. A man she knew . . .

The Viking god of her mother's stories.

Stephen Gage towered above her, his eyes tranced as he gazed at something in the distance. The room's thin light poured silver over his burnished gold hair, and his face was sheened, as though he'd walked through a drenching mist.

Lise rolled her head slightly and saw that he was staring at his own reflection in the mirror. The image was oddly distorted, almost surreal from her angle, and as she tried to bring it into focus, she began to remember what had happened . . . the turquoise inferno, the black apparition.

"Did you see it?" she asked, her words a barely intelligible whisper.

"Yes," he said.

She turned from the mirror to look at him. "What was it?"

He shook his head, still staring at the glass, lost in some shadowed dream. Gradually he seemed to realize that she was watching him, and he bowed his head, wiping the dampness from his brow, raking his shaggy hair back on his head and holding it there, as though the gesture brought him some kind of comfort.

"Are you all right?" she asked.

He looked at her then, the haunted expression gradually becoming recognition. "How are you feeling?" he asked. The silvery distance in his eyes receded swiftly to the blue she remembered, and within seconds he seemed almost normal again.

"Woozy . . . I fell."

"A bad fall. You may have cracked some ribs."

Again Lise became aware of the throbbing pulse just below her breast. She glanced at herself there, and realized several things . . . she was lying on a bed, covered with a soft cotton blanket. The room was small, dimly lit, and by the look of it, a bedroom in the Cooper cabin. Stephen must have found her by the quarry and brought her here. She had to tell him what had happened. The police should be notified—

Somehow in all that flurry of information, there was one puzzling concern that overrode everything else. Something felt wrong with her body. She brought her hand to her ribs and gingerly touched a bandage. And then she came into contact with something warm and soft. Her own breast.

It took her another moment to register exactly what was missing. Her clothes? Her bra? *She was naked!* She looked up at him, a soft gasp in her throat. "What have you done?"

"I had to . . . clean the injury. It was a bad cut."

Lise couldn't summon a response. She was trying to cope with the explosion of sensory signals flooding her groggy brain. She ran her hand down her side and felt the cotton panties. No, not totally naked, she thought, only slightly relieved at the discovery. But he'd undressed her? Dear Lord. A flurry of emotions hit her—disbelief, anger, acute embarrassment. She felt exposed and violated. She felt as wretchedly self-conscious as a twelve-year-old. He'd seen her breasts? She wanted to crawl under the blanket and die!

For another woman it might have been an overreaction. For Lise, it was the perfectly natural response of a woman who had never been seen naked by a man in her entire adult life, while unconscious or otherwise. What was more, at the ripe old age of twenty-seven, she was still uninitiated in the ways of physical love. Probably one of the oldest living virgins on the planet, she often thought privately.

"You took my clothes off? My br—" She couldn't say the word. As he nodded, the mortification hit her again. And then another emotion crept in. Fear. What kind of man was he? What else might he have done?

She tried to sit up, but the pain that stabbed at her was too intense. It ripped the breath from her lungs, and she sank back down, exhausted. Cracked ribs? Was that what he'd said? Her head swam dizzily as she imagined him doing whatever he'd done, touching her . . .

"Lise—" He covered her shoulder with his large hand, gently holding her down as he knelt beside her. "There wasn't any choice. You might have been seriously hurt. I had to find out. The cuts and bruises were bad."

Her eyes must have told him what she was thinking.

"Nothing happened," he said, his voice slightly huskier. "I don't take advantage of unconscious women."

Lise stared at him, her heart tripping. There was something so mesmerizingly intimate in his eyes, it left her speechless. He hadn't taken advantage of the situation. Somehow she knew that. But something had happened. She knew that too.

"Then what did you do?" she asked.

"I cleaned the wounds, applied an antiseptic spray, bandaged you—"

"Nothing else?" She stared at him, pressing into the pillow as she waited for his answer.

Stephen felt the movement of her shoulder beneath his hand, and it stirred an involuntary response inside him. *I didn't touch you the way you're thinking, angel eyes. But I wanted to. Like heaven and hell on a collision course, I wanted to.*

She averted her eyes at his silence, and a flush washed over her skin. The warmth of it penetrated his palm. A pulse beat frantically near the web of his thumb. He couldn't tell if it was hers, or his own.

"Nothing else," he said.

She grew quiet, the only outward sign of her agitation being the rapid rise and fall of her breathing. Her breasts moved beneath the blanket, a delicate quivering, and the awareness of it reminded him vividly that he should release her. Soon. Before his body took him on another comet ride.

As he did he saw the imprint of his palm on her skin. He could feel the constriction in his groin even as he watched the impression fade from view. The mark of a man's hand on a woman's body, he thought. His mark, on her. As her skin tone returned to normal a golden dappling of freckles appeared on her shoulder, like nutmeg sprinkled on custard cream.

He met her eyes, wondering if she'd noticed it too.

Lise hadn't seen the imprint, but she had felt its penetrating heat. And his. Something was happening between them, and she didn't have to be a sexual sophisticate to recognize the signs. It was happening because she was naked on his bed—because he was the one who'd undressed her. And it was happening much too fast.

"I can't stay here," she said.

"I don't think you've got much choice."

"But shouldn't I see a doctor?" Lise rejected that idea almost before he'd shaken his head. She knew the Shady Tree paramedics unit. Some of their children went to Abraham Lincoln, and she certainly didn't want to be rescued from the Cooper cabin in this condition. It would be all over town by the time the morning paper was delivered! No, she'd rest a little longer, just until she could leave under her own steam.

Suddenly her thoughts went off on a tangent, darting back to an unanswered question. "The rock quarry . . . those lights? What were they?"

He laughed softly, a self-deprecating sound. "Damned if I know. The electromagnetic properties are similar to atmospheric auroras, the northern lights, for example. But at this low altitude, auroral effects are usually caused by energy trapped in the ground."

"How do you know that?"

"I was sent here to study them."

"By who? Whom?" she corrected.

He rose from the bed and walked to the window, staring out into the darkness a moment. "The government. I'm a scientist."

"Really?" Lise was surprised. Beyond that she couldn't tell if she was disappointed or relieved. Of course, she hadn't ever believed Julie's wild imaginings, but she'd rather liked the illusion. And there was something otherworldly about him.

"The quarry lights aren't unique," he said, still staring into the darkness. "Similar phenomenon have been observed around the world—most recently in Norway. The theory is that they're caused by heavy deposits of ore that have been agitated by seismic activity."

"Earthquakes?"

He turned back to her. "Right. And since this is earthquake country, it looked like a chance to provide some support for the theory."

"Only? . . ."

"Only there hasn't been any seismic activity lately. So, I'm back at square one."

"These lights . . . are they dangerous?"

"If you mean radioactive," he said, returning to stand at the end of the bed, "the answer is no. The readings they generated on my Geiger counter were about as lethal as a refrigerator's."

"Geiger counter?" Remembering the static she'd heard, she stared up at him. "Then that silver creature was you?"

"That was me, the bogeyman. I didn't mean to scare you. I'd forgotten how frightening the suit can look."

"You scared me but good," she said, her laughter a heavy sigh. "I must have looked demented scrambling up that embankment."

He smiled apologetically. "Demented never looked better."

His eyes brushed over the blanket, reminding Lise that she was au naturel underneath. "Do you suppose I could have my dress back?" she asked.

"Sure, but I don't think the dress is going to be very comfortable. I can loan you one of my shirts. That should be loose enough not to bother your injuries."

A moment later he'd pulled a red flannel shirt from the mirrored dresser and was holding it up for her approval.

"Looks good to me," she said.

As he handed her the shirt they both realized the problem. She wasn't going to be able to put it on by herself.

"How do we do this?" she said, a nervous smile surfacing.

"Can you sit up?"

She tried, grimacing as the pain hit. "Whew," she breathed, settling back on one elbow. Determined, she heaved herself up again, reached for the shirt, and watched, horrified, as the blanket slid down her body. It came to rest on the fullest part of her breasts, revealing a considerable expanse of freckled cleavage. "Oh, no!"

She clutched the blanket and dropped back to the pillow, staring at the ceiling and wishing she was unconscious again!

"Here, I'll hold the blanket," Stephen announced matter-of-factly, settling himself next to her on the bed.

Lise acquiesced. It was the only way she'd ever be able to get herself clothed and decent again. With him shielding her, she managed to get her good arm into the shirt. The injured arm was another story.

Stephen watched her struggle, intrigued by her extreme modesty. He'd already seen her breasts, so he wasn't quite sure what she was hiding. But she certainly intended to hide it, whatever it was. "I could help," he offered.

"I can do it," she insisted, gasping with pain. She tried again, swearing under her breath. She twisted this way and that, wincing, moaning, but nothing worked, and finally she slumped back against the pillow, tears in her eyes. "No—I *can't* do it!"

He didn't wait for her permission. He set the blanket aside and bent over her, scooping her up with an arm around her shoulders. It was a dicey situation. There were arms, hands, shoulders, and breasts everywhere. Body parts bumped frequently, and irresistibly, before Stephen finally got her into the shirt. When at last he succeeded, she dropped back on the pillow, exhausted, her shirt lying open.

She stared up at him, blond hair flying, blue eyes tearstained, making no attempt to cover herself. The sight of her in such willful disarray was one of the sexiest things Stephen could ever remember seeing.

"Let's get this finished," he said, taking charge again. He began to button the shirt, moving with feverish determination. He wasn't doing it in deference to her earlier modesty. He wasn't doing it for her at all. The sight of her sprawled before him in total disarray was more wanton exposure than he could handle.

He started with the buttons at her neckline and worked his way down, trying his damnedest not to touch her. If she hadn't been so full-breasted, he might have succeeded. As it was, he could feel her through the shirt, and the soft shimmers of movement drove him crazy. Her body's warmth seeped through the flannel material, sensitizing his skin.

He felt an abrupt jerk of desire in his gut, and it took his breath away. It was as though someone had caught his vitals in a slipknot and yanked the rope.

She was getting to him again—the feel of her, the

sight of her. But it was the way she looked at him that delivered the death blow to his precarious state of mind. All of that sexy vulnerability and soft agony in her eyes. What did it mean? He didn't know how to read her. She almost looked as though she wanted him to take advantage of her weakened condition. What the hell, he thought, confused. She had all the dreamy urgency of a woman who wanted to be taken to bed.

What do you want, angel eyes? What do you want from me?

Lise didn't know what she wanted. She was riveted by the things that were happening to her. She'd never worn a man's shirt. She'd never had a man help her put on his shirt. And she'd certainly never had a man button up the shirt he'd just helped her put on!

No man had ever looked at her that way either.

With eyes that were silver shot and hungry. With a desire that was raw-boned and tight at the jaw. He looked as though he wanted to eat her alive. Dear Lord, he *was* a lion. Her stomach muscles pulled tight, and a Fourth of July pinwheel went off in her belly. The spiraling shower of iridescence was dazzling. It swirled like a gyro, filling her with breathless expectation. The sensation was so strange and thrilling, she didn't want it to end.

Suddenly she realized he'd stopped buttoning her blouse. His hands were poised on her body, and she could feel the weight of them against her breasts.

"Is something wrong?" she asked.

She drew in a deep breath, startling herself as she moved against him. The pinwheel showered sparks again, mesmerizing her with its brightness. She'd never felt such strange, sweet stimulation. She actually wanted his hands against her, wanted to be touched.

"What the hell," he said softly.

"Don't stop." It was a hushed invitation. Lise could hardly believe she'd said it. Glancing up at him, she wished she hadn't! A magnificent storm was gathering in his features.

She gasped softly as he bunched the flannel material in his fists and began to pull her toward him. Her stomach dipped into oblivion, a squealing child on a carnival ride. He was bending toward her, and his eyes were blazingly blue. *He was going to kiss her.*

"Stephen—" A hot stab of pain pierced her, radiating from her rib cage. "Oh-h!"

"What is it?"

She shook her head, unable to speak. A vise was squeezing off her breath. She clutched at him as he lowered her to the pillow.

"I'll get you something," he said, releasing her.

A moment later he was standing over her with a glass of water and two white capsules. "Painkillers. They're mild."

The throbbing in her side had subsided slightly, but she took the medicine without question. The pain was still intense, and she wanted relief. Sinking back into the pillow, she closed her eyes and waited for the pills to take effect. Her temples pulsed, echoing the steady beat of pain in her body.

The room hushed around her, and she wondered if he'd gone, but she didn't open her eyes.

"How is it?" he asked.

The bed moved with his weight as he sat beside her. She could feel the pressure of his hip next to hers, but still she didn't open her eyes or acknowledge him in any way. Her head was throbbing, and she needed the escape of darkness. She couldn't stand the extra stimulation of looking at him.

She wasn't sure how much time had passed before she felt the odd sensation in her scalp, perhaps only seconds. It tingled vibrantly, almost painfully, crackling across her skin like tiny spokes of lightning. Was it him? It felt as if fingers were touching her, running along her forehead, smoothing her hair.

When she opened her eyes, the pain in her temples was gone. And he was watching her, silent, an odd smile in his eyes.

Curiosity compelled her to touch him. When she did, it was just a brushing of her fingertips over the back of his hand, but the effect was the same as if he'd touched her. A shock tingled her skin, mild and pleasantly stimulating.

"What is that?" she asked.

A minute hesitation. "Static electricity. The dry weather, the equipment I use. It creates a field."

"An electrical field," she murmured, staring at her hand, fascinated as she glanced up at him. "How odd . . . my headache's gone."

She was wondering what it would be like to be kissed by a man who gave off volts of electricity, when he cupped her chin and bent toward her. Lise murmured, "I don't think we should—" And that was as far as she got.

The touch of his lips was sweetly charged and spine tingling. She tilted her head up in response, a soft sigh in her throat. Rivulets of excitement rippled through her, but more than any of the surface sensations, she could feel the kiss deep inside her, a clutch of sweet, hard need.

He said her name. "Lise . . ."

He moved his mouth over hers, and excitement prickled like a million tiny needles, stinging her lips, bringing them alive. Lise had the feeling that she was glowing, that light was spilling through her, floating clear out to her fingertips. It was the most extraordinary reaction she'd ever had. The sensations were almost metaphysical, a meditation on light where every flaw was being made perfect.

"I don't want to hurt you," he said.

Lise breathed startled laughter. That was the sweetest, most ridiculous thing he could have said. She didn't care if he hurt her. She didn't care if he tortured her, as long as he didn't stop kissing her.

A dull rip of pain spread through her ribs as she laced her arms around his neck. "It doesn't matter," she said, brushing tingly, urgent kisses over his parted lips. "Really, it doesn't."

She wanted this moment to go on forever. She wanted to savor the taste of his mouth, to be in his arms, even to know the thrill of his weight on top of her, the sweet fire of his body inside hers. For the first time she wanted to make love with a man.

And then something odd happened. Her lips began to feel prickly, as though they were going numb, and a wave of drowsiness washed over her. What was happening? The pills? "Stephen?" she murmured as her eyes drifted shut. A moment later she was sound asleep in his arms.

The darkness that enveloped the foothills that night was nearly opaque. The moon was lost in cloud cover, and even the brightest, boldest stars seemed to have burned out. Only the fire in the quarry blazed on, an eternal flame in blue.

The cabin was dark, no light emanating from its interior. From the front it looked as deserted and forlorn as it did the evening the children had discovered it. But around the back, through an opening in the shingled roof, a shaft of laser light shot into the heavens. The thin stream was translucent, the most vibrant shade of blue visible to the human eye. Its trajectory was the cosmos. Star-strewn infinity.

Inside the cabin Lise slept soundly, unaware of the bluish glow that pierced the bedroom. Behind her, the door to an adjoining room stood slightly ajar. Pulses of light seeped through the narrow crack.

A distant cry pierced the cabin's silence. Some wild creature calling out its loneliness, calling its mate.

Lise stirred slightly as the door opened behind her and blue light flared. Her eyes fluttered open briefly, a reflexive response, not seeing anything. She wasn't aware of the dark silhouette of a man standing in a halo of blue light. She didn't see him approach and stand over her.

He touched her face, and the light flowed over her, pooling in her hair. And then he drew something from his pocket, a leather pouch, which he emptied into his hand. The two stones he cupped in his palm were as smooth as agate and as black as obsidian. Their quivering energy spilled through his fingers.

Taking one stone in each hand, he stared at his glowing reflection in the dresser mirror.

And then he looked down at Lise.

Outside the cabin the quarry lights flared and the wild creature cried again.

Four

Sunshine filtered through the cabin window, dancing a path through the dust motes floating in the air and highlighting the freckles on the bridge of Lise's nose. She opened her eyes slowly, blinking away sleep. It only took her a moment to determine where she was. It was the second time in twenty-four hours that she'd awakened in Stephen Gage's bed.

This time was different, however. A man's hand was tangled in the shirt she wore. Stephen Gage was in bed *with* her.

No sudden moves, Lise, she told herself, tilting her head to check out the man lying next to her. He must have shifted toward her at sometime during the night, and the way his hand was fisted around a hunk of red flannel material made it look as though he'd given serious thought to taking the shirt off her.

Maybe he'd been dreaming? She wanted to give him the benefit of the doubt, but that possibility did nothing to reassure her quickening heart. She was struck all over again by the size of him, evidenced by the breadth of his hand, the muscular span of his arm, and everything the arm was connected to. At five feet five, she felt physically slight, almost inconsequential by comparison. If he'd wanted to take the shirt off her, he could have, she realized. Very easily.

She considered his face in repose and decided she

saw compassion there, even tenderness. He might be the stuff of Nordic legend. He might even bring to mind the warlords who stormed her daydreams and carried her off, but that didn't necessarily mean he was the sort who pillaged, plundered, and ripped bodices. Speaking of which . . .

His chambray shirt was unbuttoned, and she found it impossible to avoid the fact that his chest was drowning in a rainstorm of golden hair. Her fingers tingled with anticipation, but if she had the latent desire to touch him there, it was swiftly suppressed by the inappropriateness of such an act. She didn't even want to *imagine* herself running her fingers through a man's chest hair.

The tangled gold on his head, however . . .

She might have liked to tame that wildness a bit, or even to feel the delicious scrape of his beard against her palm.

She kept her tingling fingers to herself. No telling what might happen if he woke up and found her getting familiar with his hair. The very thought gave her chills. Instead she cautiously extricated herself from his grasp and pushed up to a sitting position, wincing at the twinge of protest from her ribs.

By the time her feet had hit the floor, she knew she was going to be all right. She wouldn't be doing push-ups for a while, but she could move remarkably well otherwise. Perhaps she hadn't actually broken any ribs. Even the cuts on her arms looked much improved, the swelling and inflammation nearly gone.

On that encouraging thought, she glanced at her watch. Seven? In the morning? Odd, she thought, moving toward the window for a look outside. The sun seemed too high for seven. A closer scrutiny told her the brand-new watch had stopped. The second hand wasn't moving. She tapped the crystal hopefully. She'd only bought the thing yesterday, so there was no possibility that it needed batteries. Perhaps she'd hit it during the fall.

Two watches in two days, she thought, turning to reconsider Stephen Gage. He could get to be expensive.

He chose that moment to make a muffled sound and reach out, gathering the blanket to him as though it were a woman.

Lise felt a wrench of something poignant. The suddenness of the feeling surprised her; its sharpness confused her. Her breathing deepened, and in the rising tumult, she recognized only one emotion, a wrench of longing. She wanted to be the woman he reached out for.

The sun was beating on her back as though to remind her that she had no business standing there aching to be held by a man she barely knew. Or any man for that matter. She had to teach that morning—and she still didn't know what time it was. She scanned the room, looking for her clothes, and as she spotted her dress draped across a chair, she also noticed an adjoining room. The closed door was warped along the frame, its white enamel paint yellowed and blistered, but it was the padlock hanging just above the knob that drew her attention.

Locked rooms had always intrigued her. Once as a child she had forced the lock on her father's study and found him berating her mother about having had an extra glass of wine that night at a dinner party. That was when Lise had begun to suspect that men were inclined to be too domineering. And perhaps too much bother all the way around.

She proceeded with caution across the hardwood floor so as not to wake Stephen. It surprised her when the padlock came open with one gentle tug. She opened the door just enough to peek in, and whistled softly at what she saw. The imposing array of equipment defied description. Even if she'd known what any of it was, she wouldn't have wanted to get within spitting distance of it. Antennae, feedback coils, wires, and cables sprang like tentacles from the bank of monitors and digital readout displays that blinked at her. The Strategic Air Command has nothing on this place, she thought.

She was working up the courage to investigate the room further when a rumbling sound caught her ear.

It was coming from outside the cabin, and growing louder by the minute. She left the door the way she'd found it, closed and padlocked, and hurried to the window.

A grimy blue Volkswagen roared up in front of the cabin and stopped, nearly disappearing in the cloud of dust it had raised. Before Lise could see clearly who it was, a pickup pulled up beside it. Oh, Lord, Lise thought, as a redheaded, denim-clad girl flew out of the Volkswagen. It was Julie.

The pickup's door panel said Frank's Gas Station, and six guys piled out of the bed. Lise recognized Buck Thompson, Frank's head mechanic, in the pack before she stepped back from the window. She'd made the mistake of dating Buck when she'd first moved to Shady Tree. It hadn't taken her long to discover the nasty sense of humor lurking behind his boyish good looks. Buck Thompson had a mean streak a mile long. Worse, he seemed to have decided Lise was his girl, and despite her polite discouragement, she'd never quite convinced him otherwise.

The gang thundered onto the cabin's creaky front porch and nearly pounded down the door before Lise could get there.

"Lise!" Julie screamed, "are you in there?"

Lise swung the door open, gaping at them in astonishment. "What are you doing out here?"

"Are you all right?" they demanded in unison.

"Of course—"

Julie bounded forward. "When you didn't show up this morning, I went over to your place—" She stopped short, staring at the red flannel shirt, her jaw dropping. "Lise, what . . . ah, happened to you?"

The men went silent, shifting, watching. Buck Thompson pressed in behind Julie, scrutinizing Lise with a dangerous glint in his icy blue eyes.

"Oh, I—" Lise surveyed her own appearance with rising alarm. She was all but naked under the shirt, totally disheveled and covered with scratches and bruises. She must have looked like one of those female combatants after a marathon weekend of mud wrestling. "I had an argument with a rock," she said.

"Wait—don't tell me," Julie said sardonically. "The rock won, right? Lise, what's going on? What are you doing out here? Like *that*? We thought you'd been abducted!"

"Yeah, where's this Gage dude anyway?" Buck Thompson had asked the question. He yanked a duck hunter's cap off his head and raked a hand angrily through his spiky butch haircut.

"Abducted?" Lise waved them silent, much as she would have her students. "Don't be silly. I'm fine—"

"This Gage dude is right here," said a voice from behind Lise. "Who wants to know?"

Silence again. Lise turned to see Stephen standing in the bedroom doorway, his blond hair looking very slept in, his shirt hanging open. If ever a man looked disheveled and sexy, Lise thought . . . At least he had his pants on!

She glanced around at the expression on Julie's face—on *all* their faces. Anger and suspicion had given way to narrow-eyed shock. Lise knew what they were thinking. She'd just told them she hadn't been abducted, so there was only one thing they could be thinking! Their prissy Miss Anderson had finally flipped out and gone nympho on them. How did she explain? This was one of those believe-what-I-tell-you-not-what-you-see situations. Maybe if she claimed she was Lise Anderson's evil twin. Like in the soap operas.

The veins were bulging on Buck Thompson's forehead, and Lise was terrified he was going to challenge Stephen to some kind of duel. However, it was Julie who stepped forward.

"What's going on here?" she demanded. "Lise, are you being held against your will or something?"

"No, she's not." Buttoning his shirt, Stephen moved into the room as though he intended to take over from there. And Lise, to her own surprise, found herself deferring to him.

"She fell last night. She was out cold when I found her, covered with cuts and bruises," he explained, congenially enough, but with a distinct don't-mess-with-me tone. As he recounted how he'd brought her back to the cabin and treated her injuries, he also admitted he'd given her some pain medication. "The dosage must have been too strong for her. She fell asleep and didn't wake up until this morning."

Julie's scrutiny of him was fiercely suspicious. She moved into the room, too, staking out her own chunk of territory.

It was a showdown, Lise thought. Julie, sheriff of Shady Tree, versus Stephen the gunslinger.

"Is that how it happened, Lise?" Julie asked, fixing Stephen with a down-the-barrel stare.

"Yes," Lise said.

"You took the pills of your own volition?"

"Of course."

"You're sure?"

"*Julie—*"

Silence as the sheriff and the gunslinger locked eyes in a staredown. *Who draws first*, Lise wondered.

"Can you drive, Lise?" It was the sheriff asking. Julie stepped up to Lise and took her by the arm as though to escort her out.

The gunslinger made his move. "I'll drive her."

"*Stephen.*" Lise wasn't sure which one she was more exasperated with. They were acting like her fifth graders fighting over who got the biggest piece of chalk. "I can drive myself, thank you both very much."

She quelled them with a don't-mess-with-me stare of her own. And then she turned her attention to the entire room. The men shifted uncomfortably. Miss Anderson was *perrr*turbed.

"I can talk for myself as well," she informed them all quietly. "And I can even dress myself, believe it or not, which is what I'm going to do now."

She brushed past Stephen without a word and pulled the door of his bedroom shut behind her. It really did astonish her how ridiculous adults could be at times. The human race was still in its infancy, she reminded herself, unbuttoning the shirt. Not long out of the caves, especially when it came to men and women. A tolerant sigh welled, and then a bemused smile. Actually, it was sort of sweet having half the town come to her rescue. Of course, now the *whole* town would know that she'd been caught in a compromising situation.

She had her good arm out of the shirt and was clumsily trying to get a snagged button free when the door opened. She turned away, clutching red flannel around her as Stephen entered. "Will you get out of here," she said under her breath. "It was bad enough before. Now you've confirmed their worst suspicions. I'll never be able to convince them we didn't—"

She couldn't say it.

He could.

"Make love?" He came up behind her. "It's not a criminal offense, making love. I don't think they'd throw us in jail even if we had."

His nearness raised the hair on the nape of her neck. Static electricity again? Or was this something else? The kind of voltage that male sexual interest generated.

"Let me help you," he said.

"No thank you." The snagged button was strangling in a quagmire of threads, and Lise seemed to be pulling the noose tighter with each tweak. "What is this, a trick shirt?" She gave the placket a good yank, prepared to rip the material if necessary. "You've got the buttons rigged or something, right?"

She kept her back to him, at war with the stubborn snarls. "Why does everything go wrong when you're around? Shopping carts, watches! Now this!"

"Lise, you *can't* dress yourself," he said softly. "You probably can't drive yourself either."

He placed his hand on her exposed shoulder, lightly at first, and then, without warning, his fingers pressed gently into her flesh. It was one of the most electrifying sensations Lise had ever experienced. She could discern each finger individually, its warmth, its length, its slightest movement. The pressure sent excitement tumbling through her.

It confounded her that a mere touch could be so riveting. Her parents hadn't been demonstrative, and she wasn't used to being touched, but that alone couldn't account for her body's bewildering response. Nerves seemed to be dancing on an electric grid just under her skin. It was almost painful.

"I don't get this, Lise," he said, his voice faintly husky. "I undressed you last night. I put this shirt on you, remember? So why not let me help take it off now? And then I'll drive you home."

His warm breath touched her neck and tickled the lobe of her ear. A jet of air riffled her hair. What was that ethereal scent, she wondered. He smelled of cedar leaves and something more mysterious. Sandalwood? Breathing in deeply, she tried to place the scent. Whatever it was, it was making her feel pleasantly light-headed and giddy.

She glanced down at the tangled button and felt herself surrendering to the situation. She would never get it undone by herself, especially with only one hand. Letting him do it made sense on a practical level, but something else was happening as well. She was surrendering to the excitement churning inside her. "All right then," she said.

She turned, her eyes averted, and let him do what he wanted.

Her imagination went wild as he worked at the button. She envisioned him taking the shirt off her, his hands brushing her skin. She even saw the moment when their eyes met and passion flared. In the vividness of her mind, he was a man gone half-crazy with desire, his hands roaming her body, his lips hot on her throat, burning a path of fire to her breasts. As the fantasy spun out of control she could feel his mouth on her, drawing on her nipples in sweet little pulls. Warm air jerked in her throat. Even the faintest possibility of such a thing happening made her nearly sick with anticipation.

"You're *not* driving me home," she whispered, her voice trembling.

His fingers hesitated on the shirt's placket, but he said nothing. A moment later he had the shirt undone.

He stepped back from her, his eyes brushing over her, taking in all the sexual signals her body was sending. The message in his darkening gaze was abundantly clear. He knew an aroused woman when he saw one. He wasn't going to press that advantage now, here, with a posse outside the door. But he would, his eyes promised. Given the opportunity, he would drive her home in every possible sense of that phrase.

The Volkswagen hit a rut and nearly threw Lise out of the cracked Leatherette bucket seat. "Slow down!" She grabbed for a wrist strap dangling above the window as Julie veered to avoid another pothole. Lise's taped ribs ached with every jolt.

"Not until I see the white line on Highway Nine," Julie vowed. "I want to get as far away from this place as possible. That guy's weird, Lise. Majorly weird."

Glancing into the rearview mirror, Julie swung off the dirt access road and onto a paved two-lane highway. Frank's truck was right behind her, followed by Lise's Cordoba, which was being driven by one of Frank's attendants.

"He's not weird," Lise said softly. "He's just different."

Julie tossed her a look. "Are you sure you're all right? You seem a little flushed to me. Maybe you ought to see a doctor."

"A doctor, why?"

"The guy did give you knockout drops, did he not? No telling what else he did."

"Julie, for heaven's sake. He didn't do anything like that."

"Oh, Lise, you're so naive. Didn't you ever see *Children of the Damned*? There were these aliens trying to repopulate their planet. They drugged the whole town and made all the women pregnant!"

Lise rolled her eyes. Julie was off and running now. There'd be no stopping the endless scenarios of alien visitations and UFO's spinning in her head. "Well, if he decides to take another shot at impregnating this earth woman," Lise said sardonically, "I hope he doesn't knock me out first. I'd hate to miss all the fun again."

Julie looked properly shocked and Lise shrugged apologetically. That was a wicked thing to say, she realized. Julie really believed Stephen *was* Darth Vader. Actually, it wasn't too hard to understand the rampant rumors. Stephen was a strange and fascinating man. Remembering the white capsules he'd given her, Lise found herself wondering what was in them. They'd been tasteless, quick acting, and powerful.

She stared out the window at the passing scenery, her imagination taking a paranoid turn. A moment later she shook her head. No, he hadn't done *that*. A woman would know if she'd been made love to, wouldn't she? Lise knew there were telltale signs, but not having ever done it before, she wasn't altogether certain what they were.

She glanced at Julie, determined not to grill a nineteen-year-old about sexual hygiene. Julie would probably be more than happy to oblige, however limited her experience, but Lise had gone to great lengths to keep that part of her life private. Even if the whole town knew she hadn't been intimate with anyone since she came to Shady Tree, they weren't privy to what she'd done before. For all they knew, she'd moonlighted at Kitten-With-A-Whip Escort Services before settling in their bucolic mountainside village.

Julie flipped the car radio on, complaining about the lousy reception as static erupted. As she switched it off, Lise remembered absently that her car radio had been acting up too. The thought got lost as Julie began to probe none too subtly for information. She wanted to know if Lise had seen Stephen eat or drink human food. She wanted to know if he'd kissed Lise, or tried anything else while Lise was conscious.

Lise assured her he hadn't, but Julie wasn't deterred. Did he stare into Lise's eyes? she wanted to know. And what did Lise think of him? Did she find him attractive, for example?

"Majorly," Lise said.

"Yeah?" Julie zeroed in on that one. "What is it you like about him? His blond hair?"

His hair, his face . . . his bedside manner, Lise thought. "That's part of it."

"He is sort of a babe, actually. So . . . if you could describe him in one word, what would it be?"

"Tactile."

"What?"

"He's very . . . tactile." A magnificent understatement, Lise thought. Stephen Gage could send out alternating currents with his fingertips. What in the world would it be like to make love with a man who had spark plugs for body parts! The possibilities made her *woozy*.

Julie had grown silent by the time they arrived at Lise's house, but when Lise reached for the door handle to let herself out of the car, Julie stopped her.

"I don't want to scare you, Lise, but I really don't think you should see him again."

"Stephen? Why?"

"You know the exhibit at the Fairchild Museum? The display of Eskimo fertility artifacts? Well, two of them are missing. The first one disappeared Sunday evening; the second, yesterday—"

"Somebody's stealing Eskimo art? Why?"

"*Fertility* statues, Lise. And it's obvious why. To gain knowledge of the mating habits of humans."

Lise heaved a sigh. "Since Margaret Mead is long departed, you must be referring to the guy who wants to repopulate his planet, right?"

"Who else? Were statues disappearing before *he* got here?"

"Julie, really—"

"*Lise*, I'm worried about you. He's picked you out for some reason. Maybe he's going to alter you genetically and turn you into his termite queen or something. You know, a one-woman breeding farm."

"Oh, thanks—"

Lise's dry comment was lost in the roar of a car engine. The pickup truck screeched to a halt behind the Volkswagen. It was followed closely by Lise's Cordoba.

Lise swung around and glared out the rear window. "I wish those yahoos wouldn't drive like that, especially with my car."

"What are you going to do about this guy?" Julie pressed.

Lise hesitated, debating that very question. What *was* she going to do about Stephen Gage? A moment later she turned to her teaching assistant and said quietly, "I'm going to ask him to help us with the class's science project."

"What? *Why?*"

"Because winning the scholarship could prove to the school board that our school has merit. That our kids don't need to be bussed to a larger community. Besides, I don't know how to build a minimetrorail, do you?"

Julie slapped a hand to her head, apparently flabbergasted. "Oh, Lord, this is worse than I thought. He's taken control of her mind."

Five

Stephen stood on the porch of the cabin, his eyes following the rutted dirt road to the place where it curved west toward the highway and was swallowed up by a tunnel of sycamore trees. Three cars had disappeared down that road several moments before, but dust continued to swirl up in little cyclones, golden devils that couldn't find a place to settle.

Restless energy, he thought, feeling a swirl of sensation in the reaches of his stomach. The woman had stirred up more than dust in her wake. She had made him restless too. He could feel it gathering inside him, creating its own faint, sweet suction, another kind of dust devil. Desire.

Irony brought a smile to his lips. The past had taught him a survival skill—self-control. He had honed it the way a bodybuilder defines his outer musculature—armored himself against emotion, punished himself. And yet despite everything he'd done, it was coming back, that raging need to make love to a woman, he'd held in check for so long. It was stealing into his thoughts, plaguing him with dark impulses.

He wanted like hell to give into it. But he couldn't.

It could destroy him this time. It could destroy everything he'd come here to do. Experience had taught him that physical desire was an illusion. The forces behind it were as seductive as the dust devil—and as deadly as the eye of a storm. He'd been caught by those forces before, and the result had been tragic.

Every sane instinct he possessed told him to stay away from Lise Anderson. Physically she was too desirable. Emotionally she was too quick to protest the slightest touch, and too transparently eager for more than touching. A dangerous mix for a man in his state of mind and body.

And yet something about her, something even beyond the physical, drew him. An odd sense of destiny struck him as he considered the risk she represented—and its ultimate implications. Perhaps the choice wasn't his to make. His mind began to stir, picking up the restless whisperings of his body. Perhaps *she* was the reason he was here . . .

He heard a rustling in the tree above him, and looked up. The sparrow hawk was perched on a limb in the uppermost branches. Sunshine brushed its head with gold and tipped its feathers.

Stephen smiled as the bird glanced down at him. "You feel it, too, don't you?" he said.

The bird's head inclined quickly, something very near a nod, and then its eyes returned to the road.

The dust devils were still moving, floating endlessly, a golden mist in the sunny breezes. The rustling that moved through the trees was a hushed sound that could have been her name. *Lise.*

Even the foothills could feel it, Stephen thought. *She was the one.*

"What happened in here?" Lise's voice was light with shock as she entered the classroom later that morning. There were dismantled cardboard boxes, uncoiled coat hangers, buckets of plaster of paris, and crumpled newspapers strewn every which way. The place looked as though it had been ransacked by vandals.

"Surprise," Julie said, grinning through the wallpaper paste that decorated her face. She swept an arm toward the table where the metrorail pike was under construction. A tiny skyscraper was listing dangerously toward a mountain range that looked like a reject from Picasso's cubism stage.

"What is that?" Lise asked, and then she answered her own question. It was Malibu, *after* the mud slide.

"It's Los Angeles!" the kids cried in unison.

"Of course, I should have known." Lise managed a faint smile. It was her own fault. Julie had dropped her off at the house to change her clothes and had gone on ahead to hold down the fort until Lise got there. Lise vaguely remembered suggesting that Julie get the kids started on the layout for their project. It was supposed to be a model of the Los Angeles freeway system, through which their metrorail would run.

Lise had thought that cutting, pasting, and papiermâchéing would be a harmless enough diversion—the perfect pastime for twenty restless little minds. Foolish woman. It looked as if they'd taken a wrecking ball to the classroom.

"Hi, Miss Anderson!" Danny Baxter hollered at her from the back of the room. He was mixing a fresh bucket of wallpaper paste to the consistency of heavy cream, and the circle of kids gathered around him were deliriously tearing paper towels and toilet tissue into confettilike strips.

The strength to endure, Lise thought, that's all she asked.

She was trying to figure out where to start the salvage operation when she noticed how much fun the kids were having. By the look of them they'd probably eaten more paste than they'd slapped onto the wire screen forms, and they were definitely sporting more construction paper than necessary for the metrorail pike. One boy had toilet paper trailing behind him. Another had a "Personals" ad stuck to his cheek. But there was no question about it. They were having a high time of it. She couldn't remember the last time she'd seen Danny Baxter laughing like that.

"Come on, Lise," Julie said. "We need bodies!"

"Help me get my lipths unstuck, Mith Anderson," someone mumbled from behind her. Lise turned to see little redheaded Susie Laudermilk muzzled by a patch of dried paste.

Susie was a nonstop talker, and Lise was toying with the idea of leaving her lips temporarily disabled when a loud crash sounded behind her. A glance over Lise's shoulder confirmed her worst fears. One of the confetti makers had stumbled into the glop Danny was stirring.

When you can't beat 'em, join 'em, Lise thought.

She rolled up her sleeves.

By the time school let out that afternoon, Lise was as grungy and paste smeared as the best of them. Working as a team, they'd made impressive strides with their futuristic vision of Los Angeles, and although she was sure most Angelenos wouldn't have recognized their fair city, she was proud of the kids' progress and told them so.

She and Julie were recruiting a cleanup crew when Lise felt someone tugging on the back pocket of her jeans. She turned to see Emily Baxter's wide gray eyes staring up at her in alarm.

"Look out the window, Miss Anderson," Em whispered, her voice shaking. "They got him!"

"Got who, honey?" Lise bent down to steady the little girl.

"The spaceman. The sheriff's got him across the street at the museum!"

When Lise arrived at the museum, she had to fight her way through the curious throng that crowded the marble steps of the proud old Georgian mansion. By the time she'd pushed past Harley Pomerance, the dog-catcher, and several waitresses from the Rib-Eye Restaurant, the crowd began to take notice of her and give way.

"It's Miss Anderson," someone whispered, "let her through."

As the human sea parted for her she saw the reason for their avid curiosity. Stephen Gage was surrounded by the gang of roughnecks from Frank's station. As usual, Buck Thompson was the leader of the pack, making wild accusations and agitating the crowd. The rest of the men were taunting Stephen with verbal gibes and threats, much as a pack of hyenas might bait a cornered lion. And Stephen looked every inch a great golden cat who didn't know which way to strike out first. He also looked as if he could do great damage if he did strike.

"What's going on here?" Lise demanded.

Sunlight flashed off Stephen's hair as he saw her. "Stay out of this, Lise. I can handle it."

"He's a damn thief!" Buck spouted.

"That's right." Billy Cornmesser appeared, dangling his brand-new stainless steel handcuffs. Billy had just been sworn in as a deputy sheriff of San Bernardino County, and he took his new responsibilities very seriously.

"We've got ourselves a coupla' missing statues, Miss Anderson," Billy said. "And this fellow's the prime suspect."

"Why?" Lise asked. "What did he do?"

"Well—let's see now. I think somebody saw him hanging around by the back of the building. Isn't that right?"

He looked around at Frank's boys for agreement, and it took Lise all of ten seconds to figure out what was going on. Buck Thompson and his cohorts were spoiling for some trouble, maybe even a public hanging. Buck obviously saw Stephen as a rival and was determined to get rid of him one way or another. The museum theft had provided him with the perfect opportunity. He'd probably even convinced Billy to detain Stephen.

"Got any evidence, William?" Lise asked.

"Evidence, ma'am?"

"Did you see him steal the statues?"

"Well—no, ma'am."

"Did anyone see him steal them? Or find the statues on his person?" Lise glared at Buck for good measure, and then she swept the gathered crowd with her eyes,

folded her arms, and delivered a stern look. "Did anybody see him steal *anything*?"

"Well, not exactly."

A great deal of mumbling ensued, both from Frank's
boys and from the onlookers. She ignored them all.

"Then I suggest you let him go, William," she said.
"Unless you want a false arrest suit on your hands."

"Wait a minute." It was Buck Thompson who
stepped forward. "What do we know about this guy?"
He jerked a thumb in Stephen's direction. "Who is he?
Where did he come from? And what the hell's he doing
up at the Cooper cabin?"

One of the waitresses spoke up hesitantly. "There is
something strange about him, Miss Anderson," she
said. "He made the wall clock stop *dead* over at the
Rib-Eye Restaurant."

Lise tossed her head. "Now, Mindy, that clock's so
old a good sneeze could stop it dead, and you know
it."

"The digital clock in my car's brand-*new*," a woman
in the crowd countered. "And it stopped running too.
Just yesterday."

"Our TV's gone haywire!" a kid called out. "Maybe
he's giving off weird vibes and jamming the circuits."

A wave of buzzing excitement swept the crowd, and
suddenly everyone seemed to have a malfunctioning
appliance.

"My damn car radio don't work!"

"And what about them UFO lights out at the
quarry?"

"Yeah!" several of them cried at once. "What about
the lights?"

It was getting out of hand, Lise realized. She sensed
a building panic among the crowd that had to be
defused before it turned into mass hysteria. She
glanced at Stephen and saw his head lifted in frozen
agony, his eyes strange and unfocused. Fear flashed
through her. Something was wrong with him, terribly
wrong. He looked caught in a nightmare, like that
night in the cabin when she'd awakened to find him
standing over her.

She turned back to the crowd, determined to distract their attention from Stephen and keep it focused on her. "Listen to me now," she said, crying out over the excited babble. "Listen to me, *dammit!*"

They quickly grew quiet. No one in Shady Tree had ever heard Miss Anderson swear before. Or yell for that matter.

"There are no UFO's out at the quarry, do you hear me? Someone made that up, and I'll admit it's a rousing good story, but it's not true. There are *no* UFO's at the quarry—and there are no lights either."

A mumbling of protest went up, but Lise persisted. She disliked having to lie about the lights, but she also knew her reputation for honesty might be the only thing that would silence the crowd and put a quick end to the craziness.

"I'll tell you what you'll find out at that quarry," she said. "*Rocks*, folks. There's nothing there but rocks. Harry Barnes"— she turned to one of Frank's gas jockeys—"did you see anything strange at the Cooper cabin when you were out there this morning?"

"Just you, Miss Anderson."

"Don't be smart, Harry."

He shrugged. "I guess not then. Nothing strange."

Somewhere inside of Lise there was a profound sigh of relief waiting to be released. She glanced over at Stephen and saw that he'd raised a hand to his head, as though he were coming out of it, reorienting. *Thank Heaven,* she thought.

"All right then," she said, addressing the crowd, her voice rising with conviction. She *was* doing the right thing. "You heard Harry. And any one of the other boys here will tell you the same thing. There's nothing strange going on out there."

The "boys" didn't look terribly happy about having been recruited in the service of Stephen's defense. But Lise didn't give them a chance to protest. She worked her way through the pack of men to where Stephen stood and hurriedly hooked her arm through his. "Come on," she said. "I'm going to get you out of here."

"I'm all right," he said under his breath. "Introduce me to your friends."

Lise glanced up at him in surprise and saw that his blue eyes were blazing with life again. They told her to do what he'd asked. No, they commanded her.

"Uh . . . Mr. Gage is a geologist," she said, turning to the crowd, "and I'd like you all to meet him. He's on vacation here in Shady Tree, collecting rocks. And now that you've been introduced, I know you'll treat him with the same courtesy that we extend to all our visitors. Why, this town is known for its winter plum pie and its southwestern hospitality."

The winter plum pie part was true, anyway.

The crowd eyed both Lise and Stephen warily. Lise could hear the stir that went through their ranks, the low buzz of conversation. Their reaction now would either make or break everything she'd done.

The silence extended until a child tugged her mother's skirt and whispered, "Where's his green antenna, Mom? You know, like the postman said."

The crowd began to titter and laugh.

Bernice Davenport, a plump, hennaed matron and the town's librarian, came up first. "Glad to meet you, Mr. Gage," she said shaking his hand. "Oh!" she squeaked, "I just got a little shock."

"The dry weather," Stephen suggested, irony in his tone.

Bernice's twin sister, Eunice, followed almost immediately. Both women fluffed their salmon-pink hair and batted their eyes at Stephen quite outrageously as they invited him to drop by the library and browse through their books on mineralogy.

"I'd like that," he said smiling.

For the next few moments Lise scrutinized the man she'd just rescued, relieved to see that he was back to normal and doing his part in all of this—the Norse god thing—an effortless kind of noblesse oblige that was quite charismatic. He did steal one's breath away, she thought, watching him charm all comers. She'd been right to interfere.

There were several among the spectators who didn't

come up, and some who continued to grumble under their breath through the whole episode. Buck Thompson and the rest of Frank's boys slunk away like jackals deprived of their prey. Still, Lise was reasonably satisfied. She'd set out to defuse the situation, and she'd managed that much.

As the rest of the crowd began to disperse, Lise called after them, "Now, you're all going to stay away from the Cooper cabin, aren't you? It's private property. Mr. Gage rented it, fair and square, and he deserves his privacy just as the rest of us do."

Lise had no idea how Stephen had come to be staying on the Cooper property, but she was determined to add an air of legitimacy to his being there.

Finally there was no one left on the marble steps but Lise and Stephen. The few actual patrons of the museum who were drifting in and out did little more than eye them curiously.

"Are you all right?" Lise asked, searching him with her eyes. His features revealed nothing, none of the trancelike confusion she'd seen earlier, none of the agony. She had so many questions to ask him, and all the answers seemed to be stored in the depths of his gaze. Deep space, his eyes. It was so easy to see why people were afraid of him. He wasn't quite human somehow. He didn't seem to have a normal man's flaws, and yet she suspected he carried a flaw that ran far deeper than any normal man.

"I'm fine," he said at last, shrugging off her concern. "I get headaches now and then." He seemed to be studying her features as a slow smile formed. "It's just that I've never been rescued by a woman with paste on her face."

She touched her own cheek and felt a scaly patch. She'd never been overly concerned about her appearance, but the thought of making public speeches with white blotches all over her face was a little disconcerting. "I didn't know. Nobody said anything."

"They were probably afraid to. You're pretty ferocious when you're angry." He shook his head at her and laughed. "You lead a dangerous life, lady. I don't think

I've ever seen a woman get herself into as much trouble in as little time. And I always seem to be the cause."

It took her a moment, but she managed a smile. "Just so I know . . . are you planning on getting me into any more trouble, Mr. Gage?"

They both went silent, struck by what she'd just said.

The flash of intrigue in Stephen's eyes was breathtaking. "Maybe . . . I hope so."

Warmth crept up Lise's neck. The air was so thick with anticipation, she could breathe it. And him, she thought. She was breathing him. A low wave of sensation caught her, weakening her legs as if she were standing thigh-deep in water. Lilacs, fresh cut grass, and a ghosting of sandalwood drifted on the breezes.

Stephen rallied first, saving the moment by rubbing at some paste on her chin with his thumb. "I've got to be honest though," he said. "You look better in red flannel than you do in paste. Come on, let's clean you up."

He caught hold of her hand and pulled her along with him to the gardens that were adjacent to the museum. A moss-drenched birdbath sat unused among rainbow garlands of spring flowers, and an ivy bower lent the area an air of seclusion.

"Lovely," Lise murmured as she glanced at herself in the mirror of clear water. "Not me, the flowers. I look as though I tangled with a cement truck."

"Let me," he said as she reached to dip her fingers into the water. He tilted her chin up with his hand, wet his fingers, and scrubbed gently at the patches of white. Lise was surprised at how easily she gave in to his wishes, and how often. It seemed every time they were together, he was dressing or undressing her, cleaning her up like a child. It was a strange predicament for a woman who'd always considered herself independent. Correction, she thought, who had *fought* so hard for her independence.

"Do you like doing this?" she asked. "Baby-sitting grown women? Taking care of them?"

He smiled. "Women? Plural? I like baby-sitting you."

He was scraping softly near her upper lip. "I think I'd like doing anything to you."

A direct hit, Lise thought. The man had good aim. He got her right where she lived. Every time. She closed her eyes as he brushed his thumb over her lips. Several soft strokes. He's not cleaning paste anymore, she realized. He's touching me. *Caressing . . . me.*

I ought to stop him, she thought. *But I don't think I can. I like it too much. I like what he does to me.*

Lise wasn't the only one who didn't know if she could stop.

Stephen could feel the quiver of her mouth beneath his fingers, and it paralyzed him for a moment. She fascinated him with her softness and her seeming willingness. He could feel the turmoil in her when he touched her. He could feel her need to resist, and then something happened . . . a softening in her body and in her breathing. It tore him up, that sighing moment of abandon when she gave up the fight, when all the resistance went out of her, and her lips parted.

There was something he had to tell her, something important, but he couldn't resist the way she responded to him. As his thumb pad brushed the silk of her inner lip, its delicacy brought other, more erotic images to mind . . .

His stomach tightened, hollow again, alive with sensation. He drew his hand away, and her eyes flew open. Her sharp intake of air was like a fist to his ribs. She looked dazed and softened, still totally vulnerable.

Say what you have to, he told himself.

"Lise—" He cleared the huskiness from his throat. "You did the right thing at the museum. Telling everyone there were no lights. I don't want anyone endangered until I know exactly what's causing the aurora, do you understand? I don't want anyone out at the quarry."

There were questions rising in her eyes, a quick flash of uncertainty. She had doubts and fears, he realized, but she was suppressing them. She wanted to be talked out of them. Her shoulders lifted slightly, then dropped with the breath she exhaled. "Sure," she said after a moment, "I understand."

Lord, he thought, she could stop a Mack Truck with those eyes. Fascinated, he watched her lips part again. Her tongue darted nervously along the inside edge, reminding him how warm she was there, how delicate. He imagined how her lips would feel, all that shiny softness against his mouth. And suddenly he knew he had to do more than imagine.

There was a pulse in her throat as he rested his hand there, and he could feel the same faint pulse beat in her lips when he bent to take them, gently.

The sound that breathed out of her made him want to be tender with her. His hands trembled slightly, responding to an impulse stronger than anything he'd felt in years. He had a deep, *raging* need to be tender. But there was also another urge kindling inside him, the hellfire of sexual desire—and the colliding impulses sent a current of energy straight to his groin. As the deep aching began he knew he would be ready for sex within moments, as ready as he'd been in the cabin. But this . . . was just as impossible a predicament. He was mentally prepared to deal with the impulse this time, but the setting was wrong. They were out-of-doors. They were in a park, he reminded himself. Even if she was willing, it was broad daylight.

He broke the kiss and threw back his head with a ragged breath, half laughter. A moment later he looked down at her.

"Does that mean good or bad?" she said.

"*Good.* And too bad we're in a park."

She laughed, and for some reason the silvery sound of it alerted him. He looked beyond her and saw a gardener watching them. Then he noticed through the bowers that the side windows of the museum had eyes. "I think we're under surveillance."

"I'm not surprised," she said. "The wonder is they're being fairly discreet about it." She glanced through the trailing ivy, half-laughing, half-sighing as the silhouettes disappeared. "I think you have an image problem, Mr. Gage."

"You have magnificent powers of observation."

She looked a little smug. "I know how to solve it. You just need to let people see you in a normal role."

"And you have a normal role in mind?"

She ignored his faint sarcasm. "Why don't you come by my class tomorrow and give my fifth graders some tips on their science project. They'd love it, and it would give them a chance to get to know you."

"A science project?" One of his golden brows arched ironically. "The sacrifices a man has to make for his image."

Long wisps of blond hair had escaped from the coil at the nape of Lise's neck, making her look wistful and lovely. He smoothed them back, and she laid her cheek against his hand as he drew it away.

It was a seemingly guileless gesture, but breathtakingly seductive. It also seemed totally out of character, and he found himself wondering if it was a spontaneous caress. Or if she'd done it before, with some other man. And then he realized he knew almost nothing about her. There didn't seem to be any way to approach the topic of her romantic past, so he brought up a more immediate problem. "This town's pretty protective of you, aren't they?"

"Very protective," she agreed. "Look what they did when they thought you'd abducted me."

He smiled. "I wonder what they'd do if I actually did it. Abduct you."

Her eyebrow lifted. "That's assuming I'd let you."

"That's assuming you'd have a choice."

She drew up, an arch in her posture. Her long, graceful neck was a swan's curve, and her eyes sparkled like melting diamonds. Stephen realized he'd challenged her, and as much as that possibility intrigued him, a second awareness intrigued him more. He'd also aroused her. Her gaze was darkening, and her breathing had quickened.

Shame on you, Miss Anderson, he thought. *You've just told me exactly what you'd like me to do.*

Six

Stephen stood in the darkness of the cabin's living room, staring out at the full moon. Floating just beyond the zenith in the western sky, it was as potbellied and luminous as an oriental rice paper lantern. He massaged his temples and pulled out a chair from the wobbly dinette table that was pushed up against the windowsill. It was three in the morning and he hadn't slept.

A leather-bound logbook lay open at the far end of the table. He dragged it to him and switched on a light as he sat down. The blank page stared up at him like a stone tablet waiting for divine inscription. He released the pen that was clipped to the book's spine.

Omega Mission, Day Five, he scrawled. *Failure to establish contact again. Nine days left to achieve successful transmission of data, otherwise mission will be aborted. Source of failure unknown at this time. Dosimeter levels indicate "solar proton event" is intensifying. Time is critical, and yet I must wait another twenty-four hours before I can try again—*

He set the pen down and pushed the journal away. Light seeped from the storage room door behind him, and a sudden high-pitched signal caught his attention. The shrill beeping drove him out of his chair.

The darkened room was alive with activity as he pushed open the door. Red light pulsed in the gloom, a vibrant heartbeat against the steady drone of electronic circuitry. He strode past digital readout displays beaming intermittent status signals and a bank of monitors that projected extraterrestrial images of earth. The distress signal came from an oscillograph that was spewing out ribbons of data. He hit the reset button and silenced the machine.

Just moments before he had set every device in the room on Self Test. Time was his enemy now. He had to find the glitch, especially if it was in his own equipment. There was always the possibility that the problems were in the ship orbiting out in space. If that was the case, there was nothing he could do. Years of effort would be lost, and the damage to Omega Mission incalculable. But he didn't believe the problems originated with the spacecraft. They were right here. The problems were his.

He scoped the pulsating room with his eyes. Where was the failure? The geomagnetic storm building in the earth's upper atmosphere was far more intense than he'd predicted, but the system was specifically designed to withstand such electrical interference. And yet *something* was jamming the transmission. He might have been able to rule out sabotage, except for what he'd discovered that morning. She had been in this room. He'd inadvertently left the door unlocked the night she showed up, and the next day he'd found it locked.

Lise's clear eyes and serious smile shone in his mind like sunlight breaking through clouds. He could see her as sharply as though she were standing before him. She was that kind of woman, expressly self-defined and free of ambiguity. Somehow he knew he would always see her in his mind that way, with such clarity of detail that it would seem as though she were there. It was ridiculous to think that she would do anything to hurt him, he realized. There wasn't a devious bone in her body. She was scrupulously honest, a principled woman. What was more, she couldn't possibly know why he was actually here—or what he was trying to do.

He could feel a tightness at the base of his skull as he scanned the array of sensors one last time. The room's harsh reddish glow, its pulsing lights seemed to be flashing inside his head. A dull pain throbbed behind his eyes, warning him that it was lying in wait—the white noise, the oblivion that routed his senses. He had no heart for solving the puzzles his equipment presented that night. The ship wouldn't be within range again for another twenty-four hours, a frustrating detail that gave him great gaps of time between transmissions. Time! He had too damn much of it now—and too little overall. At the moment he needed to breathe, to clear his head.

The night sky was devoid of stars as he walked out onto the porch. An owl hooted softly in the distance, a forlorn sound that knifed through him. This place was lonely. The vast wasteland he'd come from hadn't felt as desolate as these hills did. There'd been nothing there he wanted. Nothing to remind him he was a man.

The stricture in his throat might have been laughter, only it was too acid. Too harsh. She'd changed all that. She'd reminded him that he was something lower than a man, something closer to an animal in rut. Lord, the pain of that night he'd had to undress her.

The sycamores stirred, whispering her name . . . *Lise.*

He descended the porch steps into the darkness, breathing in cool air, trying to calm the sudden hard rhythm of his heart. What was it about her? He was drawn to her, inexorably drawn. It was more than physical. And it was testing his control.

His stomach muscles tightened on their own hollowness, reminding him how empty he was. It was a sensation he'd come to associate with her, only now the pulling inside him was vibrant, almost painful. It felt as though all of the electrical impulses in his body were being drawn toward his groin, draining the energy from his limbs, from his brain. The eye of the storm, he thought, the vortex. It was wild and lonely, that empty feeling. As lonely as an animal calling out its need.

He needed the woman.

The claws of sexual longing ripped through him. Gut-deep and beautiful. *Beautiful.* His jaw muscles knotted as he fought the sensation, willing away the hardening in his loins. But he couldn't stop it. It was her that he needed, the coupling of two pounding, aching bodies. *Deep, aching sex.*

His body throbbed with the need for physical release, but it was so much more than that. He needed her for life. She was his way out of the darkness. She could give him back everything he'd lost—and everything he'd thrown away.

Laughter again. Harsh. Acid. All of this yearning was insane, he told himself. He knew nothing about her. She might have someone else, a lover. His intuition answered that doubt immediately. She didn't. The flashes of yearning in her eyes said she felt it too. She'd felt the claws.

The price then. *Every dream had its price.* What was the cost of wanting her? Even if she meant him no harm, there were others who did—on her behalf. Buck Thompson wanted to kill him—or at least do some serious damage. The man had violence in his eyes. Stephen understood the allure of violence. It was as cleansing as it was destructive. It was cathartic. He might even have welcomed a confrontation under other circumstances, but his mission was already at risk.

Some dreams were too costly, he told himself. Even if he begged, borrowed, and stole to have her, what then? Would making love to her be enough? He could never take her where he was going. And he could never leave her behind.

"Which of these screws is an RH two dash fifty-six by five sixteenths?" Julie called out. She was bent over the parts to the model train kit they were hoping to "customize" into something resembling a metrorail system.

"You're asking *me*?" Lise was laboring over the railroad pike, trying to align a series of tiny telephone poles along a highway.

"I think we're in over our heads," Julie grumbled. "Couldn't the kids just grow something in a petri dish instead?"

"Not if we want to win that fifty-thousand-dollar scholarship money. If we don't show up at the science fair with something that looks like a metrorail, we haven't got a snowball's chance."

Lise glanced out the front windows as the cries and whistles of playing children drew her attention. Summer school had let out for the day, but as always, several of her students lingered on the playground.

She rolled a telephone pole absently between her fingers. She truly enjoyed the sounds of children playing. Their familiar shouts were a form of security somehow, almost a comfort. But it wasn't the antics of her students that kept her gazing out the windows so intently.

She'd been preoccupied for the last two days over the possibility that Stephen might show up. *Preoccupied*, she thought, that hardly covered it. Forty-eight hours of thinking about little else but the moment when he would walk into her classroom. She was hung up, stuck in the groove like a cheap record needle. What was worse, when she wasn't contemplating his arrival, she was wondering why he *hadn't* arrived.

All morning she'd felt drawn to the windows. Once or twice she'd even found herself gazing out toward the hills, in the direction of his cabin. She glanced down at the object she was rolling in her fingers and clicked her tongue softly. Freud would have a field day with this, she thought, setting the telephone pole down. It wasn't in her makeup to be so quixotic. She wasn't the type to tilt at windmills or go off on romantic tangents. And even though she probably harbored a fantasy or two, she'd never been led by them.

"Earth to Lise—"

Lise picked up the telephone pole and redoubled her efforts. "What is it, Julie?"

"You okay?"

"Sure—I just can't get this thing to take root."

"Maybe you need some glue." Julie pushed the instructions aside a bit too eagerly. "I'll get it."

"You read," Lise countered. "I'll get the glue."

What greeted Lise inside the storage cabinet—in addition to the regular supplies—was a bowl of petrified papier-mâché, several piles of wadded construction paper, and two opened tubes of glue, both of them nearly squeezed dry. Someday her students would learn the difference between a storage cabinet and a wastebasket.

"Off to the supply room," she called to Julie, who was still mumbling to herself over the instructions.

Lise slipped the supply room door key off its hook and shut the cabinet. She'd barely left the classroom and entered the corridor when she saw a figure step out of the gloom at the end of the hall. Her intuition told her who it was as she strained to make out the shadowy features of the man who was walking toward her.

"Stephen?" His name slipped out under her breath. He couldn't possibly have heard her. There was a flashing energy about him that was almost visible as he walked up to her. It put her instantly on guard.

"What are you doing here?" she said.

She wasn't sure what made her more apprehensive—his silence, or the blazing concentration of blue in his eyes as he stopped and stood before her. His gaze swept over her body with the intensity of a spotlight, leaving her feeling as though she'd been searched without ever having been touched.

She repeated the question softly, reaching for a breath. "What *are* you doing here?"

"I thought I'd been invited," he said.

"Oh, yes . . . well, school's out for the day. The kids are already gone."

"I didn't come for the kids, Lise . . . I came for you."

"For me?" Her throat went dry, and her heart went wild. "What does that mean?"

His eyes touched hers, and their searchlight intensity narrowed, probing, penetrating her thoughts. "You know what it means."

"No . . . I don't."

His eyes darkened then, reproaching her. "This isn't like you, Lise. It's not in you to lie, even to yourself."

But I lied for you, she thought. *I told the museum crowd you were harmless—a tourist—when a part of me sensed they were right. You are different, and frightening.* Lise looked away, her heart pounding. Why hadn't she listened to her own doubts and fears about him? Had she been too busy defending him? Or had she suppressed them? Either way she was acting like a woman who didn't know her own mind.

"I came for you, Lise . . . to be with you."

His voice was taut and sure and rivetingly male. There was such certainty in it, such latent power that she felt a strange weakening of her will, almost a giddiness. He knew what he wanted and for some reason that thrilled her. He'd come for her. *He'd come to make love to her.* She couldn't let that happen, of course. It was too crazy even to consider, but that didn't stop her from going weak-kneed at the thought.

He touched the collar of her white linen blouse, almost as though to straighten it, but his hand lingered and drifted down the lapel, grazing her breast. His thumb lifted the edge of the top button. "You know why I'm here, don't you?"

She held in a sigh, and its energy trembled down her body. Even though she shook her head imperceptibly, she loved the heat of his hand against her. It was dark and concentrated, like his eyes. The vibrancy of his fingers, the thought of what else they might do, sent strokes of anticipation radiating through her.

"*Lise* . . . answer me."

She looked up raggedly, her control ebbing away. "*Yes,* I know why you're here."

He released her then, leaving her swaying in his wake as he scanned the corridor and spotted the supply room door to his right. Darkness spilled into the hallway as he opened the door and turned back to her.

"We can't go in there—"

But she let herself be drawn into the room with him, her heart rocketing as he closed the door behind them. She relinquished the key without protest, watching it glow in the dim light as he locked them in. The only illumination came from a narrow fanlight window above the door. *Why in the name of heaven didn't she stop him?* She didn't understand the frightening control he had over her. Or why she was breathless and trembling when she ought to be resisting.

Something was driving him, too, she realized as he turned back to her. There was just enough light for her to make out the tension in his features as he reached out and touched her face. His fingers were rigid as they traced her jawline, leaving her skin tingly and numb.

"You have something I need," he said.

"What—"

His eyes flared, incandescently blue. His jaw gripped painfully. Breathing a four-letter word, he took one slow step toward her, caught her under the arms, and lifted her to him, his palms pressing into the sides of her breasts. *"This.* I need to touch you again, Lise. Like this. I need your breasts under my hands, your lips under my mouth. I need you flat on your back, your beautiful legs spread—"

"Stephen!" She was so shocked, she couldn't say anything else. He had jolted her back to reality. *He had jolted her with rioting, slamming excitement.* She wanted to stop him. She wanted to *slap* him, but her hand didn't seem to be getting the message!

Light from the window streamed above them, arcing halos through his golden hair. He was strong and sure, his hands hot on her body. Despite the thundering noise of her pulse, Lise was aware of so many things at once. The inherent fear of relinquishing power, the seductive thrill of losing control. She could feel strength racing through him, flowing into her. His palms were pressed into a softness that had ripped painfully alive in just the last ten seconds. It was as though he'd pulled a lever and turned on a paralyzing current. The shock was running through her body, grounding her to the floor.

"Let go of me—" The words spilled out helplessly.

"I can't do that, Lise." His dark eyes were shadowed by a hunger that made her stomach knot. "I can't let you go. Don't you know that?"

There was something odd and vulnerable in his voice, a ragged quality underlying the raw desire. It was almost sad, and it drained her of every ounce of resistance.

She tilted her head back, and felt a pulse throbbing wildly against the arc of her neck. She didn't know what to do. She didn't know how to stop the crazy impulses flooding her senses. He was going to make love to her right here if she didn't stop him. Was that what she wanted? The burn of his lips on her throat. The slow wonder of his hands. The hard thrust of a male body. *Was that what she wanted?*

The answer came with a gush of dampness between her legs. Lise Anderson, who'd never had a man in her life, was about to have her first in the supply room of Abraham Lincoln Grade School. She must be straitjacket crazy.

"*Sigh*, Lise—" He said the word as though he'd found some new meaning for it. "Sigh for me." And then he caught hold of her chin and brought her mouth to his. As his lips moved over hers she discovered for herself what the word meant. She felt as though the pit of her stomach had gone to liquid, as though a warm pool of silvery sensation welled inside her. There was a sweet heaviness in her legs that weakened her balance and jumbled her thoughts. It was fluid and honeyed, that heaviness. Her body was softening, it was *sighing*.

He stroked her face with his fingers, deepening the kiss.

She was dissolving. If he kept this up, she'd cease to exist beyond a shimmering tide pool of sensation.

The pool rippled and swirled as she closed her eyes and opened her mouth to him, returning the kiss. She felt as though she were welling with life, and yet there was another awareness that was even more insistent. It was deeper, tighter, the urgent throb of female need.

He broke the kiss and gripped her by the shoulders.

His voice was low and urgent against her ear. "*Lise*, Lise, I need you now, here, up against this wall. I need your legs wrapped around my waist. Give me that, Lise. Give me what I need."

Her answer was an audible sigh, a draining sigh.

He pressed her against the wall and began raising her skirt, the pressure of his hands electrifying her. His fingers felt as though they were scattering sparks all over her skin. Somewhere in the distant recesses of her brain, she knew what was happening to her was crazy and reckless, that she would probably regret it. But that knowledge was too faraway to grasp. It was a piece of driftwood caught in an outgoing tide, receding from view with every wave of sensation that passed through her.

"You're shaking," he said, stemming his assault on her clothing. His breath held a groan as he brushed her temple with his lips. The kiss was taut, feather-light. "What is that, Lise? Need? Tell me it's *need*."

"I don't know . . ."

Disbelief rocked through her as she glanced down at his hands on her bared legs. For a moment it seemed as though she were looking at someone else's body, another woman who was half-naked and melting with desire. And then a tremor began in her thighs that she couldn't control. It seemed to come from somewhere deeper, her very bones, and it rolled up her spine until she was quaking with a violence that felt as if it might never let go of her. "I don't think I can do this—"

Stephen caught her by the arms to steady her and Lise clutched at his shirt as another tremor shook through her.

"Lord—I'm coming apart here," she said brokenly. "I'm sorry—" She couldn't explain what was happening, except that it had to be a delayed reaction. The sight of her own hiked-up skirt had thrown her into some kind of identity crisis. *Lise Anderson was doing it in the supply room?* It was more than her over-wrought nervous system could handle.

"I *can't*," she said, fighting tears of confusion. "I should never have . . . I don't know what I'm doing in here."

Stephen held her back a moment, as though he were trying to convince himself of her need for creature care. She must have looked dreadful because he pulled her into his arms with a harsh sound and held her steady until her trembling finally began to calm.

Lise was immensely grateful for his ability to shift gears, and a little surprised. Moments before he'd been the conquering army. Now he was a sheltering force. His arms felt like a haven to her shocked sensibilities. He was warm and substantial, exactly what she needed. Resting her head on his shoulder, she breathed a sigh. Everything might have been perfect if only, through the deep, steady rate of his breathing, she hadn't heard a clatter of footsteps in the hall outside the door.

"Lise?" Julie called. "Where are you?"

Lise started to respond, but Stephen clamped a hand over her head, pressing her into his cotton-knit sweater. "She'll never find us in here," he whispered.

Lise shook her head, mumbling through muscles and fabric. She gasped as he freed her. "I told her I was going to the supply room!"

The doorknob jiggled violently.

Stephen released a faint groan.

"Lise? What are you doing in there?" Julie demanded. "I found some rubber cement."

"That's great!" Lise called back. "I'll be another couple of minutes. I'm hunting for a—" She swung around and searched through the shelves, spotting something she actually needed. "For a *tape measure.* Listen, why don't you call it a day, Julie. We'll hit it again tomorrow, okay?"

"Are you all right, Lise?" Julie persisted.

"I'm fine. Go ahead, take off. I'll see you tomorrow."

"Lise? . . . Why is this door locked?"

"Locked? No, it's jammed, you know how it always jams. Go on now, Julie. Go *home*."

"Oh, yeah . . . okay. See you tomorrow then."

As Julie's footsteps faded into the distance Lise began automatically to adjust and smooth her clothing. The trembling had receded to a fainter inner vibration by the time she got her skirt twisted around right and her blouse tucked back in. It was suddenly, vitally, important to her that she recover her sense of order, her sense of self, and anything else she might have lost in the abandoned interlude.

When she turned back to Stephen, she was Miss Anderson again, Shady Tree's indomitable grade school teacher, role model and guardian of the public morals. The only trace of the "supply room wanton" was in the wispy disarray of her blond hair and a smear of lipstick on Stephen's shirt.

"Saved in the nick of time," she said. "Both of us."

Stephen regarded her darkly. "Speak for yourself. I didn't want to be saved."

"We both know what *you* want," she informed him.

He smoothed back the flyaway strands of hair that had strayed onto her face, his fingers lingering and sensual. Though the wildness had receded, a glint of the hunger remained in his eyes. "And I know what you want," he said.

"You do? And what is that?"

He touched a finger to her lips. "Show-and-tell, Miss Anderson. One of these days I'll surprise you."

Seven

"*Wow!* How'd you *do* that?" Danny Baxter cried. His little sister, Em, stood next to him, clutching a time-worn Tiny Tears doll as she watched the man at the front of the class in rapt silence.

"It's a magic jar," another student whispered.

"No, it's a magic paperclip!"

Lise stood at the back of the classroom, watching along with her students. All eyes were riveted on the "magic show" being performed for their entertainment and edification that afternoon. Even Julie was watching Stephen Gage's sleight of hand with total fascination.

Inside the glass jar Stephen held, a large metal paperclip floated in thin air. Drifting like a helium balloon, it was held down by the piece of string that was taped to the bottom of the jar.

"What would you say if I told you there was no magic involved?" Stephen asked the children.

"What else could it be?" Em asked softly.

"Well, maybe this jar is filled with antigravitational space." He went to Em first, giving her a closer look, then walked through the aisles so the other children could see. "Or maybe there's something else at work here. Another force of nature called magnetism."

Lise smiled to herself, every bit as taken as the children by the handsome sorcerer in their midst. Only it wasn't Stephen's magic tricks that held her spellbound, it was his personal transformation. Yesterday in the supply room, he'd been dark and dangerous, a blue-eyed demon from hell. Today he was Buck Rogers, hero of television reruns and every child's friend. Today, freshly shaved and wearing the red flannel shirt, he could have run for mayor of Shady Tree and won. There was simply no trace of the mesmerizing darkness. She actually felt a little pang of regret at not having met him when they were younger, perhaps in high school. What a prom date, she thought.

Lise and Julie exchanged a knowing smile as Stephen took the jar apart and showed the children the magnet he'd taped to the lid that was attracting the paperclip. The kids reacted with "Ohs" and "Ahs."

"I knew it all along," one of them boasted.

Stephen enthralled the class with several more magic tricks that afternoon, using each as an opportunity to explain some of the fundamental elements of science. It was one of the most effective teaching tools Lise had ever seen. He'd said he planned to surprise her, and he had.

As he brought his act to a close the class broke out in applause. Lise walked to the front of the room, applauding too. "Thank you, Mr. Gage. That was wonderful. Wasn't that wonderful, class?"

Wryness softened Stephen's smile as he inclined his head. "My pleasure, Miss Anderson. But didn't you say something about a science project you wanted me to look at?"

"Yeah!" the children exclaimed.

Lise indicated the model railroad pike they'd all been working on diligently. She winced as Stephen walked over to the half-finished layout. Seeing it through his eyes, she realized what a truly sorry-looking affair it still was.

"Well, what do you think?" she asked, joining him.

The class watched them silently.

"You're going to need more than magic for this," he said, lowering his voice so that only Lise could hear. "You're going to need a miracle."

By the time class was over that day, a miracle was in the making. Rather than put the train together with the kit instructions, Stephen came up with a fascinating alternative. He suggested the students forego electricity as the train's sole energy source and use electromagnetism instead.

He explained the theory of electromagnetic propulsion in terms they could understand and described how the West Germans were using it to run their new "magnetic levitation" train. And then he used his paperclip trick to illustrate the levitation aspect.

"See how the magnet attracts the paperclip, lifting it into the air," he said, passing the jar among them. "In a 'maglev' train, there are permanent magnets in the train's undercarriage that are attracted to the steel in the guide tracks above them. The attraction lifts the entire train into the air."

"That's *so* rad!" Danny Baxter said.

Stephen smiled at the boy's excitement and tossed Em a quick, conspiratorial wink. "It's like a magic carpet ride."

As the class began to barrage Stephen with questions, he called them around the pike, answering their inquiries as he explained how to modify the train and the tracks to achieve the levitation effect. Everyone crowded around eagerly, including Julie.

Lise felt a little left out, but as she observed the children's enthusiasm, she realized how successful her idea had been. They not only accepted Stephen, they were fighting to stand next to him. She watched for a time and then glanced out the window. The school yard was deserted except for an elderly woman making her way across the stretch of pavement where the kids played basketball. The woman's wayward shopping cart was loaded with groceries, and every once in a while, she stopped and gave the front wheel a good kick.

A private smile stirred as Lise remembered her first meeting with Stephen. She was too much the hard-headed realist to believe in fate, and yet if she hadn't picked that gimpy cart, they might never have met.

He'd made a powerful first impression—hair the color of winter sunshine, eyes like deep space.

She turned back on impulse, intent on stealing another glance at him—only Stephen was nowhere to be glanced at. She scanned the pike and then the entire room, but there wasn't a sign of him. He was gone! Julie and the kids were so intent on making a railroad car "levitate," that Lise hated to interrupt them, but her curiosity wouldn't be stemmed.

She pulled Julie aside quietly. "When did Stephen leave?"

Julie looked around, obviously unaware that he had. "Beats me," she said, mystified. "Must be another of his magic tricks—the vanishing act."

They both laughed, but Lise was still perplexed. If he'd needed to leave, why hadn't he said anything? Why disappear? Especially when she was just beginning to think of him as a regular guy. She needed a second opinion.

"What did you think of him, Julie?" she said, aware for the first time of her assistant's starry-eyed smile.

"Me? I think you should hunt him down and marry him immediately," Julie blurted in a soft burst of laughter. "He's not only majorly gorgeous, he's brilliant."

Lise was astonished. "Are we talking about the same guy that you thought was here to repopulate his planet?"

"If that's what he's here for"—Julie flashed a quick little salute—"sign me up."

Stephen was parked in his black Land-Rover across the street from the school when Lise left that afternoon. He watched her walk to the parking lot, appreciating her steady, graceful gait and the way her breasts swayed beneath the blush tones of her sweater.

He liked her, he realized. That probably wouldn't have surprised him if he hadn't been so totally absorbed by the physical attraction raging between them. Somehow he'd missed the heart of her, the essence. His chest tightened and the unexpected reaction made him draw a breath. She was the quintessential schoolteacher, devoted to her kids, generous to a fault with her time and energy. He liked her strength and self-reliance. He liked her incredible warmth.

The only thing that puzzled him was why she wasn't married to some adoring guy and raising a passel of kids. She did have one hell of an independent streak, he decided, smiling. Maybe that explained why suitors weren't lined up at her door. Their loss, he thought. They obviously didn't know what he knew about her . . . that underneath her buttoned-to-the-neck blouses and efficient manner lay a fantasy, *an abandoned fantasy.*

As her Cordoba sailed past him Stephen hit the ignition key and pulled out, following her at enough distance so that she wouldn't be able to make him out in her rearview mirror. He was counting on the fact that she would be heading home. Lise Anderson didn't strike him as a woman who went out dancing after work. But then there were many things he didn't know about her.

A short time later she pulled into the driveway of an older two-story home with a shingled roof and an expansive front porch. There were camellias in the front yard and bramble roses climbing on green latticework. The place was right, he thought.

He watched her let herself out of her car, straighten its lopsided hood ornament with a quick tap, and walk to her porch. That was right too. As she disappeared inside her house he smiled again and pulled the keys from the ignition.

Shady Tree's schoolteacher wanted to be abducted. He would try to oblige.

Lise undressed slowly, with an altogether different sense of herself than she'd ever had before. She felt alert and aware, responsive even to the air around her. If someone had told her her skin was glowing, she wouldn't have been surprised.

She pulled her sweater over her head, folded it with practiced care and deposited it in a lilac-scented drawer in her dresser. Just as children's laughter gave her comfort, it gave her ease of mind to know that everything was in its place. She felt as though she was contributing a little bit of order to a disorderly world.

Had she gained weight? She considered herself in the mirror as she kicked off her woven leather flats, then unzipped and slipped off her skirt. Her breasts were spilling out of her bra, but her hips still looked fairly trim. Lord, but she felt ripe, like a peach about to fall off the tree.

When she was naked, she glanced at herself again. It was something she never did, and a faint tingling raced across her shoulders and down her arms. Her breasts flushed and peaked, and her thighs felt tight. There was also a telling moistness in her nether regions that made her vaguely uneasy, but she rather liked the rest of it—the tingling, the vibrancy.

A jangle of bells surprised her. Someone was at her door.

She quickly slipped a white eyelet nightgown over her head and grabbed her matching robe, wondering who it could be. She never had unannounced visitors.

There was no one there when she opened the door.

"Lise . . ."

The voice had come from her left. As her eyes darted over the porch she saw Stephen Gage sitting on the railing near a large, clay-potted Dieffenbachia. He was wearing the same jeans, red flannel shirt, and leather jacket he'd worn to her class that day. Even in the falling light, his eyes were blazingly blue.

Lise caught her robe together. "What are you doing here?"

"I was hoping for something more like 'it's great to see you, Stephen. Why don't you come in?' "

She glanced at the Dieffenbachia as though for protection, absently aware that something was wrong with the plant. The bottom leaves were yellowing and wilted, even though she'd just watered it. Pot bound? she wondered, distractedly.

"Lise? Are you going to invite me in?"

"I'm not *dressed.*" She met his gaze reluctantly, knowing what she would see there . . . shadings of quizzical humor, of intimacy, very male. "All right, so you've seen me wearing less," she admitted. "It's still a little awkward entertaining in your robe."

"Then don't entertain me. Just invite me in."

Not only was Lise out of comebacks, she wasn't sure why she was resisting the idea of inviting him in. She wanted him in. At this very moment there probably wasn't anything else in the world she wanted more. Still, she was apprehensive. He was an unpredictable man, overpowering under any circumstances, and being alone with him was certain to lead to a close encounter of one kind or another.

"Perhaps we could talk," she said, holding open the screen, "once I've changed."

"I like to talk." There was a studied casualness about him as he crossed the threshold.

She followed him into the living room with the distinct feeling that she'd just been invaded by the enemy, *at her own invitation.* She couldn't help wondering what he was thinking as he scanned her carefully preserved furniture with its rich flowery brocades. She'd bought it secondhand.

Stephen wasn't thinking about her furniture at all, except that, like everything else about her, it seemed to fit. He was still reacting to the effect she'd had on him when she'd opened the door. Wisps of blond had escaped her French braid, and in the white peignoir, she'd looked like a princess bride on her wedding night. Dressed for a fantasy, he thought.

"I didn't get a chance to thank you for coming by the class today," she said, relaxing her hold on the robe's drawstring bodice. "The kids loved it, and you really boosted morale. We might even have a shot at the prize money now, thanks to you."

He regarded her with interest. "Winning that contest seems very important to you."

"It is." Glad of the opportunity, Lise explained about the possibility of the grade school's conversion to a community center. "I want to show them that the students at Lincoln are learning important things, and *doing* important things," she said. "Winning a national scholarship couldn't hurt."

He seemed impressed with her efforts. "You've got the reason and the passion," he said. "Now all you need is some luck."

"I think *you're* our luck." She flushed with laughter as their conversation drifted off into an uneasy silence.

Lise wanted to suggest that they sit. She wanted to offer him something to eat or drink as she would have any other visitor, but this wasn't a social call, she could tell. He had some specific purpose in mind. "You didn't come to talk about the science project, did you?" she said.

When he didn't answer, she persisted, though every reasoning instinct she had told her not to. "Yesterday you said I had something you needed."

"I did say that."

"Is that why you're here . . . tonight?"

"That's part of it." The setting sun glowed golden in the windows, and his eyes were luminous in the falling light.

"But don't worry," he added softly. "I'm not going to drag you into a supply room and ravish you."

Lise reclaimed the robe's lapel. "Thank goodness for that."

"I've got something else in mind."

"You do . . ." Her throat went chalky and dry. A throw rug bunched under her bare feet as she edged away from him. "Would you like something to eat? Or to drink?"

"No thanks."

"Are you sure?" she said, continuing to put distance between them as she backed from the room. "I've got some Anjou pears in the cooler. They're delicious. I'll get some cheese. And wine." She reached the archway to the kitchen and waved him back. "Sit down! I'll just be a minute."

The Brie in her refrigerator looked a little grayish, so Lise grabbed some crackers to go with the pear slices. A bottle of California chardonnay she'd picked up at the supermarket wasn't chilled, but she took it anyway.

Whatever he had in mind, she thought, loading up a tray, he would be doing it on a full stomach. Maybe that would slow him down until she could get some clothes on.

The front door was hanging open and there was no sign of Stephen anywhere as she returned to the living room. She called out his name, set the tray on the coffee table, and walked to the door. It was rapidly growing dark outside, and a ripple of alarm moved through her as she scanned the yard. "Stephen?"

She didn't see his Land-Rover parked out front, and remembering how he'd disappeared from her classroom that afternoon gave her an uneasy feeling of déjà vu. If this was some sort of cat-and-mouse game he was playing, she wasn't amused. Surely he didn't think that sort of silliness was exciting to a woman.

She ventured out onto the porch and down the steps, alerted by the soft rustlings in the grove of aspens alongside her house. A sudden breeze fluttered her cotton robe, but she doubted it was the wind making that noise. It sounded more like someone moving among the bushes.

"Stephen? Is that you?"

The small grove glittered with moonlight and shadows. Somehow Lise had managed to reach adulthood with remarkably few fears, but anything that went bump in the night qualified. It was only the niggling doubt that something might have happened to Stephen that kept her moving cautiously toward the trees.

The breeze gusted and the rustle of leaves became an eerie rush of silver thunder. Lise's senses quickened as she paused at the periphery of the grove. She thought she'd heard a voice through the noise, someone calling her name. "Stephen? Is that you?" Peering into the darkness, she moved along the border of the grove. Each tree seemed to spring to life as the passed it.

The wind breathed her name again and she hesitated, her heart quickening as she turned in the direction of the sound. She scanned the trees and saw the silhouette of a man standing in the heart of the grove. Moonlight cast a silvery nimbus around the darkened form.

"Stephen?" she called.

The silence frightened her. She wasn't close enough to discern whether it was actually a man, or just a shadow, but it was ominously still. The wind was silent as she edged closer, every instinct heightened. A crackle of sound to her right raised the hairs on her neck. She whirled, and heard someone come up behind her. A shadow fell across her path, and her heart ripped out of control "Who's there?"

The breezes swirled her hair, and she caught the scent of something familiar, sandalwood.

"Stephen, if that's you—"

"I've come for you, Lise."

Thunder roared in Lise's ears, the wild silvery thunder of a thousand trembling leaves. She closed her eyes and the sound filled her senses, cascading through her like water, breathing with her body. It was a lullaby, a symphony driven by brass and woodwinds, and in its clashing closing notes, Lise heard someone speaking to her. Stephen. He was telling her not to be afraid, promising not to hurt her. . . .

"Do as I say, Lise. Do you understand? Do exactly as I say."

Her breath caught in. "What are you doing?"

"I'm taking you with me, away from here."

"Where? Why?"

The wind whistled softly, darkly. It lifted her skirt with breezy, questing fingers.

"You wanted to be abducted—"

"What . . . ? I never said that!"

"You didn't have to say it, Lise. I could see it in your eyes. You wanted to be swept away, transported."

"No—" Her breath shook in her throat.

"Lise. Do as I say. Take off your robe."

His voice was low and male, hypnotic. She closed her eyes, trying to shut him out, but the soft command resonated through her. It was as powerful as a physical touch. It probed into vulnerable places, weakening her nerves and calling up all the riveting sensations she'd felt in the supply room. A sweet, frantic helplessness stole over her, and suddenly her heart was laboring in her chest.

"What are you going to do?" she said.

"Everything you want me to do. Everything you've ever dreamed about."

Dreamed about? How could he know that? She'd never told him her dreams. Her fantasies as a young girl.

"Take off the robe, Lise."

"I can't." She *couldn't.* Her arms and legs felt like leaden weights. Her heart was a crazy weightless thing, beating somewhere outside of her. She didn't have the strength.

She felt his hands run down her arms, easing off the robe in one fluid, effortless motion. The dull rip of cotton fabric made her wince as he tore off a strip of material. "What are you doing?"

"It's for your eyes—"

"A blindfold? No!"

He caught her hand as she brought it up, restraining her gently. "I'm taking you to a place you've never been, Lise, a place where we can touch the stars. I want it to be a surprise."

She let out a trembling, disbelieving sigh. "I don't like surprises, Stephen. I've *never* liked surprises."

"Sure you do." A telling wryness softened his voice. "You're just a little afraid of them."

"A *little* afraid? Stephen, I'm petrified!"

He let out a soft groan of something that might have been laughter and drew her up against him, gentling her with his voice and his hands. "It's all right, Lise," he said. "Nothing will happen that you don't want to have happen. This is your dream."

Her dream . . . Lord, wasn't she the one who secretly believed some dreams had to be shared to come true! Well that explained it. She'd tempted fate.

"I'm not going to hurt you, Lise," he said. "I'd never do anything to hurt you. Do you believe me?"

His voice was mesmerizingly husky. His hands were strong and bracing, *so warm on her arms*. Lise could feel his breath lifting her hair, sighing with sandalwood. *Believe* him, she thought, controlling the hysterical sound that bubbled inside her. She didn't believe any of this! What was he doing to her? And why was she so gloriously weak, she could hardly stand up?

"Lise . . . do you want me to do this? Tell me now if you don't, and I'll stop."

The answer that swept into her mind was no. *No, this was much too enthralling a dream for a woman who'd lived a life of careful restraint. No, she couldn't. No, she shouldn't.*

"I want it," she said finally, her heart surging.

His chest rose with a harsh breath. "The blindfold is a gift," he said. "Welcome the darkness."

The fabric dropped over her head, and as he knotted it loosely, her thin nightgown swirled around her, belling out with the air currents. *A gift?* Lise sensed some elusive meaning, but her thought processes were too scattered to make sense of anything at that moment. She felt naked without her robe, and the rising heat of his touch made her dizzy and breathless.

He released her then, standing back as the wind breathed silver lullabies, and the leaves trembled above her head. Her mind went crazy imagining what he might be doing. Was he looking at her? Could he see through the nightgown?

She heard another rip of fabric, and her heart went wild.

"Give me your hands, Lise. Put them behind your back."

Lise wouldn't have believed it if someone had told her that this sort of thing could ever have happened to her. That a man would come into her life this way, a strange and powerful man who could make her do things she didn't believe she was capable of. A week ago she wouldn't have believed it.

"Your hands, Lise. I won't tie them tightly . . . this is part of the dream."

A sound rose in her throat as she unlocked her clasped fingers. It was a shocked and trembling sigh. Her body arched instinctively as she put her hands behind her back, and he looped the fabric once around her wrists. *What was she doing?* What was she letting *him* do?

"Everything you ever dreamed of, Lise."

Leaving the material draped over her wrists, he swept her up in his arms, moving so quickly, she was forced to press into him for balance. He covered what seemed like a short distance, perhaps fifty feet before he stopped. A car door creaked open and he lifted her into the seat.

Moments later they were roaring down the highway.

Lise was in a state of shock and wonder. Her world had gone dark, and yet she was acutely aware of everything that impinged upon her—the slightest swerve of the Land-Rover, the needlelike prickles of the upholstered bucket seat, the rubber floor mat vibrating beneath the balls of her bare feet. Her sensibilities were heightened to the point of pain. Even the delicate hairs on her arms pricked like sensors.

Though she couldn't see Stephen, his image stood out in her mind like a photograph. She was riveted to his every movement, to his shifts of weight and posture, to his occasional, audible breaths. If she could only read his mind. *If she could only predict his actions.* He had promised he wouldn't hurt her. On a rational level, she was sure he meant it. And yet she felt totally out of control.

It was the ultimate irony, she thought. *It was her karma.* She'd spent a lifetime avoiding physical intimacy with a man. She'd always believed that some ancient territorial instinct took hold once a man made love to a woman. He became possessive and autocratic. Her father had controlled nearly every aspect of her mother's life, and the possibility of that kind of relationship had always terrified Lise. And yet, now, with this man, the loss of control was thrilling somehow. *Why?*

Gravel ground out under the wheels of the Rover,

and Lise swayed back against the seat as they lurched up a steep incline. The car kept climbing and climbing until finally she was afraid they would topple off the edge of some mountain peak.

From somewhere beyond them a crow's raucous squawking carried over the drone of the engine, and the wind roared against the windshield, but there were no specific sounds to tell her where they were.

"Why can't I see where we're going?" she asked.

"There is nothing to see. Yet," he added.

When they finally came to a stop, Lise pitched forward, gasping as a brawny arm broke her fall. He pressed her back against the seat with one powerful arm swing, crowding her breasts. She could feel heat and muscle through her nightgown. She could even feel the hair on his arms.

"Are you all right?" he asked, concern in his voice.

Before she could answer, his door had wrenched open and slammed shut. A wall of cool air hit her as her own door opened, and she was scooped out of the van and into his arms.

"*Lise*—talk to me. Are you all right?"

"Yes, yes—fine," she said, "just out of breath."

Moments later she could hear the sound of solid granite beneath his feet, the crunch of pebbles as he carried her toward some unknown destination. They were climbing again, she realized. She burrowed into the warmth of his leather jacket as a gust of wind whipped at her hair.

He pulled the open jacket around her, covering her against the night's sudden chill. The air that penetrated her eyelet nightgown felt cool and sharp against her flushed skin. Occasionally she caught the scent of something she vaguely recognized—pine needles or brown, sun-dried sage—before it was carried away by the wind.

It was his scent that enveloped her as they climbed toward what felt like the zenith of the world. The tangy odor of his leather jacket mingled with the musk of overheated muscles and a tantalizing hint of something that might have been sandalwood.

"Where are you taking me?" she asked.

"I told you, Lise. To a place you've never been, a place where we can touch the stars."

He moved quickly and powerfully up what seemed to be the sheer side of a cliff. The image that swept her mind was a golden lion of a man carrying her off to his lair. She saw him vividly—the Norse warrior—rough in his seduction, hungry in his ravishment of her trembling body. The fantasy left her weak with anticipation, dizzy with fear and desire.

And then her imagination truly went off on a tangent. Perhaps he *was* an alien life-form, she thought, imagining some luminous spaceship awaiting them on a distant and lonely mountain peak. The thought sent a hard shudder through her. A panicky burst of laughter burned in her throat. The air was getting thin, and *she* was getting hysterical!

Eight

Stephen was breathing deeply as they reached a plateau. Lise pressed herself against him for balance as they floated downward for an instant. And then the icy wind was gone, as though they'd taken shelter in a ravine.

"We're here," he said, his breath warm against her face.

She felt herself being tilted forward and realized he was setting her down. Even though her hands weren't bound, she felt a precarious sense of vertigo. "Wait!" she cried as her nightgown began to hike up. Cool air swirled through her legs, and an instant later rock-solid ground burned the soles of her bare feet.

After being carried for so long, she felt weightless, as though she were spinning in space. With her vision gone, the disorientation was total. She stepped backward, gasping softly as she lost contact with him. "Stephen?"

The ground was uneven, studded with rocks and crevices. A moment of terror caught her as she imagined stepping off the side of a cliff. "*Stephen! Where are you!*"

"Here—"

She felt a tug at her wrists and realized he'd drawn off the cotton fabric.

"You're all right, Lise," he said, turning her around,

pulling her into his arms. "I've got you." She felt herself being lifted gently and settled back down. And then something hard and cool pressed against her back, an embankment. *Thank Heaven, solid earth.*

His hands anchored her shoulders, a steadying force. Lise slumped against the granite wall behind her, letting her head tilt back, breathing deeply. Lost in the darkness of the blindfold, she shuddered as he released her.

Several seconds passed before the trembling subsided, before she became aware of his silent presence again. "Stephen?" What was he doing now?

"You make a beautiful captive," he said.

Her nightgown felt like liquid silk against her skin, a cool flutter of nothingness. She knew it must be transparent in the moonlight, which meant he was seeing what she'd seen in her bedroom, tightening thighs, breasts that were full and overripe, a woman's body shamelessly in need of a man's attention.

He hadn't touched her in any intimate way, but she knew he was going to at any minute. In the dark recesses of her imagination, she could already feel his hands lifting her nightgown, sprinkling her thighs with electricity. "Let me go," she whispered softly, not quite sure why she'd said it. He wasn't even touching her.

He knew why she'd said it. He smoothed back her hair and lifted her chin. "I can't do that, Lise."

His voice was grainy and hushed. It had the same riveting obsessional quality she'd sensed in the supply room. She felt his warmth as he drew close and hesitated, close enough to kiss her. A quiver of excitement darted through her body as she anticipated the sweet shock of his lips.

"You said it was my dream—" The words rushed out of her, forestalling him, delaying that inevitable moment when he touched her and she went weak at the knees, weak in the mind. "That nothing would happen I didn't want."

"This *is* what you want—"

His mouth brushed hers lightly and all of her protests fell away. Her chin trembled. Her lips parted, tingly and urgent. She could even feel warm air streaming gently through her nostrils. It was happening again, she realized. That same glorious softening that came over her whenever he touched her. Her stomach went to liquid as she tilted her head back, yielding to him.

She said yes to the deep, draining kiss she expected.

But he didn't kiss her. Instead he did something far more alarming, something wildly thrilling to a woman as inexperienced as Lise. He took hold of her hands and pressed them to the wall behind her, one on each side of her head. The unexpectedness of it left her shocked and breathless. Granite cooled her shoulders, making her aware of the heat that came off his body. She felt weakened, nearly paralyzed by the implicit power of what he'd done, and yet he hadn't hurt her. He wasn't even touching her except where his hands held her.

"You want to be swept away, Lise," he said. "Transported, *taken by storm.*"

His thighs brushed against hers, and the flare of his body heat called up an answering flare from deep within her. It fanned out from the pit of her stomach and swept through her senses so suddenly, she couldn't breathe. It seared the back of her throat with a sharpness that wouldn't let her swallow.

"Stephen—" A helpless sound constricted in her throat. She caught at his arms, intending to push him away, but the gentle nudge of his hipbones caught her loins on fire. If she'd had any doubt that he was made like a normal man, it vanished the moment she felt the evidence of male arousal against her thigh. The dawning awareness arrested her thoughts. In the space of a heartbeat, she was riveted by the hardening wonder of the male body, by the slow burn of it against her flesh. Stephen Gage might not be human, but he was fully capable of making love to a human woman!

"You want a man to make you tremble and sigh, Lise—"

His hand stroked down her arm, trailing a shower of sparks in its path. As his palm came to rest on the small of her back, Lise moved against him involuntarily. She couldn't help herself. Some irresistible tidal rhythm pulled at her.

He caught her by the hips and brought her up against him, letting his hands slide down to her buttocks. "You want it all, Lise. *You want to touch the stars.*"

A grainy sound wavered in Lise's throat. This wasn't a dream, she realized. This was sexual seduction. These were the ancient overtures to taking possession. He moved against her, pressing into her softness, and desire flared. It swept through her like a wind-fed fire, burning sweetly.

She resisted the terrifying pleasure of it for an instant, and then she slumped against the wall and let the flames take her. The fight was lost. It was useless to struggle against what was happening. He was too powerful. He wasn't a man, he was a force of nature.

"You *are* a beautiful captive," he said, tilting her face up to his. His hand was warm on her throat, a slight waver in his touch. "And this *is* what you want. It's what I want too."

From somewhere a voice cried out to Lise to give him what he wanted . . . *whatever he wanted.*

He took her lips at last, electrifying her.

Her mind flashed a vision of the kiss, of lips touching breathlessly and bodies coming together. Against the dark landscape of night, she saw a man and a woman surrounded by an aura of shimmering green light. Their embrace was incandescent, one of the most beautiful things she'd ever imagined.

She wanted that beauty, with him.

"Stephen—" She reached out blindly, touching his face, his hair. Her voice broke softly. "I do want this . . . I want you."

There was a shudder in his breath as he gathered her up in his arms. She could feel his heartbeat, and the sudden urgency of his embrace. This wasn't seduction anymore, she realized. It wasn't a dream. It wasn't even sex. He was shaking. *He needed her.*

"No—not this way." She pulled at the blindfold, trying to free herself. She wanted to look at him and touch him. To make it real. "I have to see you."

He unknotted the cotton strip, and as it fell away from her eyes she saw a dark form swimming in stars. "Move into the moonlight," she said urgently. "Let me see you."

He took her by the hand and brought her around with him. As the light struck his features she saw the chiseled bones take shape and the golden hair flash with silver.

"Do you believe me now?" he said softly.

"Believe you? About what?"

"About this place. About touching the stars."

He pulled her into his arms and swept a hand out toward the sky. It was true. The heavens were studded with stars that looked close enough to touch. Lise felt as though she were standing among them.

She looked up at him and saw the emotion she'd sensed. It was stored in his beautiful eyes and in the grip of his hand as he held her. "Yes, I believe you," she said. He wasn't an alien life-form or a Norse myth. He was a man, and that realization brought her another awareness. There was something he had to know about her. Something crucial she had to tell him.

She laughed softly, embarrassed. "I've never done this before."

"Never done what?"

"I've never made love with a man. I've never touched the stars." A wave of wild relief swept through her as she realized how easy it had been to tell him. The waiting and wondering was finally over. Sex would no longer be the ultimate mystery in her life. What pleased her more was that after so many years, she wasn't afraid.

"Which star shall I touch?" she said, searching the sky with her eyes. Laughter bubbled up inside her. She couldn't seem to control the delighted sound.

"Lise, this *can't* be your first time."

The low astonishment in his voice startled her. She turned to look up at him, and the laughter died in her throat. His features were changing, harshening. The emotion was becoming something else, something frightening. She couldn't tell if it was disbelief or anger.

"What's wrong, Stephen?"

His taut silence was answer enough. If there was one area in Lise's life where she was painfully vulnerable, it was the subject of her virginity. Why didn't he just say it, she thought. Mature, overripe? How ridiculous for a woman her age to be a virgin?

She was struggling for words when she saw something just beyond him in the sky. A hoary wave of darkness swept the night horizon. The clouds boiling toward them were devouring everything in their path, blotting out the stars, swallowing the moon. It looked like something out of a movie.

"Stephen—look!"

As he turned, a bolt of lightning split the sky in two. Its jagged, icy light scarred the heavens. The answering roar of thunder was deafening. Lise pressed her hands over her ears. The air was choked with the pungent stench of sulfur.

"What's happening?" she gasped.

"An electrical storm," he said, grabbing her hand. "They blow in quickly at this elevation. Come on! Let's get back to the car!"

They began to run, sidestepping rocks and crevices, dodging boulders. Stephen's eyes were fixed on the punishing terrain ahead when he felt Lise's hand wrench from his.

"*Ahhh!* Stephen—"

He whirled at her cry of pain. She'd dropped to the ground and was clasping her foot. Lord, she was barefoot! He'd forgotten. "I'll carry you," he said, scooping her up. "We've got to get out of here."

The path down was treacherously steep and hard to follow in the dark. Lightning spat at Stephen's back, and thunder roared at every turn, as though the heavens were seeking vengeance. Lise's fingernails bit into his neck as she clung to him, but her pale, beautiful features registered something closer to stoic determination than fear.

Halfway down he came upon a shortcut, a dried-up creek bed where the rocks gave him better traction. He'd barely made it thirty yards before the rain started. It was a violent downpour that drenched both of them in seconds. He gave her his jacket, but it did little good. They were soaked to the skin by the time they got to his Rover.

The drive down the mountain was equally treacherous. The rain had washed out the shoulder of the road in places, forcing Stephen to stay to the middle. He tried to use the white line as a guide, but rain sheeted the windshield, blinding him for several seconds at a time. The van shimmied and squealed as he took the corners. He was driving too fast.

He was aware that Lise was pressed back against the seat, her fingers gripping the armrest, but he hadn't realized she was staring at him until they reached the bottom. A streetlight illuminated her silent, drawn features. Her stoicism had given way to apprehension, and in the soggy nightgown, she looked like a frightened, rain-drenched waif.

"What's gotten into you?" she said, her voice faint. "The way you're driving, I'd almost think a pack of hellhounds was after us."

She's closer than she knows. "I wanted to get down off that mountain. The roads are death traps in this kind of weather."

"All the more reason to drive cautiously. Stephen—what's wrong?"

There was a shake in her indrawn breath, and it tore him up to think that she was frightened because of him. "Nothing—except that I was an idiot for taking you up there."

Her voice thinned out. "Why? Because of what I told you? That I'd never been with a man before?"

"No." *Yes,* he thought. Yes, it was that. She had saved herself with that confession. She had said the one thing that could have stopped him at that moment. The lightning storm had done the rest. Lord, he hoped it was *just* a storm.

"I'm not some trembling virgin, Stephen. I'm twenty-seven. I know what I want."

But do you know what you'd be getting, he thought. "I've got to get back to the cabin," he told her, slamming the Rover into a lower gear. The back wheels were skidding and he needed traction. "The lightning could damage my equipment, a power surge."

"I'll go with you."

"No."

"Stephen—"

"No." He silenced her with a quick, angry glance. "I'll let you out at your place, and I want you to get the hell inside and stay there, do you understand? These kinds of storms can kill people."

She went quiet then, but the hand she'd knotted in her sodden nightgown told him more than he wanted to know. He'd hurt her. Drawing in his next breath became an ordeal. He'd known this was going to happen. It was inevitable. *Why the hell hadn't he stayed away from her?* If he needed a reason not to see her again, he'd just found it. He had hurt her. He would hurt her again. It *was* inevitable. Pain bred pain.

Rain pelted the windshield, running in streams.

The storm was letting up by the time they reached her place. The lightning had subsided, but the drops were still falling hard. He pulled the van into her driveway, reached across her and opened the door. The chill that came off her damp nightgown made his heartbeat slow and painful. "Can you get inside by yourself, Lise?"

"I can get in." She shrugged off his jacket, refusing his help.

He made no more attempts to help her as she slid to the ground. He didn't trust himself to touch her. Barefoot in the rain in her nightgown, he thought, his chest tightening. What would the good people of Shady Tree think if they could see their Miss Anderson now?

He pulled the Rover out and swung it around.

She stood in the grass alongside the driveway,

watching him, her eyes puzzled, angry and sad, her hair curling damply around her face. She looked like a water spirit who had wandered too far from her enchanted lily pond.

He waved at her to go into the house. *Why the hell didn't she?* And then he hit the gas and pulled out. A fiery pain flared through his jaw as he glanced in the rearview mirror. She was still there, standing in the pouring rain, watching him roar out of her life.

With a giant heave, Lise pulled the Dieffenbachia free of its terra-cotta clay pot and set it on the porch.

"Just as I thought," she said, heaving a shaky sigh. *"Pot-bound."*

Its roots were twined around the root ball in a dense, suffocating mass. The plant was strangling itself. Lise wiped at her dripping nightgown frantically, oblivious to the mud and dirt stains on her hands as she crouched to prune the tangled artery network.

The fibrous tendrils were no match for her flashing stainless steel knife. Lise imagined she could hear screams with every amputation, but she never wavered until the job was done. There was nothing more important to her on this night of abductions and electrical storms than to get the plant where it could live and breathe.

A short time later she stood in her yard in the drizzling rain, staring at the living thing she had just liberated. The Dieffenbachia stood, stunned but proud, near the driveway.

Grow, baby, grow.

She walked back into her house without once looking at the road Stephen Gage had taken moments before. When she reached her bedroom, she yanked the soiled nightgown over her head, dropped it on the floor, and stared at herself in the mirror. She was wet and bedraggled and dirty. She looked like a drowned cat with breasts.

"What does he know." Her voice hoarsened with

pain. "There are men who would kill for this overripe body."

A feedback signal beeped softly and insistently in the predawn stillness. Stephen awoke with a start. The flashing lights and zigzagging readout displays bewildered him for a minute before he remembered where he was.

He sat forward in the straight back chair he'd fallen asleep in and massaged his aching temples savagely. It was all right, he reminded himself, calming his rising panic. The equipment hadn't been damaged. Once the worst of the storm had subsided, he'd even managed to make contact. The transmission had been only seconds in duration, but it was a breakthrough nonetheless. Now, the question was, could last night's communication be repeated? He still had to prove it wasn't a fluke.

The storage room was stifling as he left its whirring activity and walked to the bedroom window. Dawn was sheening the hills with pink and gold. It was going to be a beautiful day, he realized, but the awareness brought him no joy. He wouldn't be seeing too many more California sunrises. He would miss the austere beauty of the hills. He would miss her.

Was she still standing alongside the road?

The image was indelible in his mind. The Rain Maiden. Wistful and wounded. She probably thought he hadn't wanted her, that *she* was inadequate in some way, when nothing could be further from the truth. He was the one flawed.

Pain thrust at him like a dull knife blade, as blunt and tearing as the moment he'd let her out of the car. It had nearly killed him to leave her that way.

Was she awake now? Was she getting ready for school? Sitting in a shaft of sunshine? Braiding her hair?

He should have told her it was him. He should have told her about the other woman—the one he'd stupidly talked into intimacy before either of them was ready—

with tragic results. He owed her an explanation, at least.

Rising light turned the window into a mirror which captured every detail of his haggard expression. *This is no less than you deserve, Gage,* he thought. *Wanting her is your punishment. Letting her go is your atonement.*

He turned away from the window.

"Tah*dahhh!* The train of the future!" Julie's hand cut a flamboyant arc through the air as she presented the class with their masterwork, the model maglev train.

Lise stood at the back of the room, her stomach tied in knots as the class waited breathlessly for Julie to throw the switch. The project was far from done, but this was their first test of the electromagnetic propulsion system and it was crucial. They'd all been working furiously, even giving up their weekend to get it ready. They were using the electric induction motor that Stephen had helped the children assemble the day he'd spent with them, but he hadn't been around to help them with the magnetized reaction rails.

He hadn't been around period, Lise thought. A hot sensation, like a branding iron, touched a nerve in her cheek. She hadn't seen him since the storm two nights before.

"Conductor, ma'am?"

Lise gave Julie a quick nod. "Hit it, Chief Engineer."

Julie approached the switching mechanism with great flourish. "A drumroll, please," she said.

The class obliged, and as their clattering fingers subsided, Julie executed one last Carnack-the-Magnificent bow.

Lise actually felt a stab of panic as Julie put her finger to the switch. There was so much at stake. Beyond winning the scholarship money, even beyond losing the school, there was Lise's own personal need to have this system work. She couldn't call on Stephen for help again. She *wouldn't* call on him for help.

"Julie! Stop kidding around and do it," Lise pleaded.

Startled, Julie threw the switch.

The silence was deafening. No lights, no choo-choo noises, no nothing. Their masterwork didn't.

"Aw, shoot," someone moaned.

"It's a dud!" came another outburst.

Lise gave way to the panic rising inside her. "Is the transformer plugged in?" she called, rushing up the aisle toward Julie.

Julie ducked behind the table for an instant. "Yup, everything's plugged but the toilet."

Lise hushed the class's burst of laughter and tried the switch herself. Not a hiccup. The system was door-nail dead.

"I think we need the Maytag repairman," Julie said, grimacing. "Where is Flash Gordon, anyway?"

"Yeah, where's the spaceman?" Danny Baxter asked.

"He's *busy*." Lise fished through her tool apron for a screwdriver. She removed the plug from the wall socket, then loosened the lid of the switching mechanism and removed it, perusing the wires. She had gotten quite good with a screwdriver in the last couple of days.

"Lise," Julie persisted, obviously perplexed, "let's give Stephen a call."

"*No*. Absolutely not!" Lise caught herself. The kids were staring at her like she'd grown horns. "We'll fix it somehow," she said. "We *will* get this heap running before the science fair, if I have to tie a string to it and drag it behind me."

The class was silent, including Julie.

Miss Anderson was *perrr*turbed about something.

Hours later, all by herself in the empty classroom, Lise contemplated her mechanical nemesis—the little train that *couldn't*—and wanted to cry. It wasn't a question of finding someone to help at this point. There probably wasn't anyone in Shady Tree who'd ever heard of magnetic levitation, much less understood the dynamics behind it. She and her kids were on their own with a high-tech white elephant. It was too late to start another project, and without the train, they were sunk.

"Miss Anderson?"

Lise turned to see Danny Baxter in the doorway. He had a hand propped against the door frame, and he was breathing hard.

"Something's wrong with my sister," he said. "I think she's sick or something. Could you come over to the house?"

Lise felt a jolt of alarm. She'd been so distracted, she hadn't realized that Em Baxter hadn't come to class that day.

Lise wasn't surprised by the shabbiness of the Baxter place as they pulled up in front of the house. She knew Danny and Em's mother had been struggling to make ends meet since the divorce. Danny had told her on the drive over that he and Em were alone much of the time since his mother had taken a second job in the evenings. "Sometimes I cook dinner," he'd said proudly.

The urgency Lise had felt throughout the drive increased as they entered the house.

"This way," Danny said, leading Lise down a narrow hallway to a bedroom at the back of the house. A set of bunk beds and a fiberboard dresser were the room's only furniture. It took Lise a moment to determine that Em was the lump under the blanket on the bottom bunk.

Lise knelt beside the bed, and pulled back the cover.

"Em?" she said softly, soothing the child's brow. Her pale face was flushed with color, but it was the unhealthy stain of a fever. Lise's first impulse was to call a doctor immediately, but she would need to know Em's symptoms.

Em's eyes drooped open and her lips pursed slightly. A smile, Lise thought. A wan smile, but nevertheless, it was one of the few times Lise had seen her do such a thing. She felt immediate and almost irrational relief.

The little girl had always been special to Lise. Perhaps it was because her own stable, predictable world was unraveling at the seams. Even the quiet, bucolic nature of Shady Tree seemed to have been altered in some way she couldn't define. And yet this somber child was inviolate in Lise's mind. Em Baxter symbolized something gentle and vulnerable Lise felt the need to protect at any cost.

"Tell me how you feel, Em. Where does it hurt?"

"My stomach," she said.

Danny fidgeted next to Lise, fairly bursting to be heard. "She got sick over at the park when we were playing," he said. "She upchucked and everything!"

As Lise probed Danny for more information she felt Em's forehead again. The fever didn't seem to be dangerously high, and with luck, it was just a bout of the flu, but Lise didn't want to take chances. She was going to notify Danny's mother at work and then call a doctor. The child would have to be watched to be sure it wasn't something serious.

An hour later Lise had Em propped up with pillows and sipping some ginger ale to help settle her stomach. The doctor had assured Lise over the phone that there was a new strain of twenty-four-hour flu going around, and that with some bed rest Em would be fine.

"Take two aspirin and call me in the morning." Lise tapped the reddened tip of Em's nose and laughed. "That's what the doctor said, so I guess you're going to be okay. How are you feeling now?"

After a moment's contemplation, Em quietly pronounced herself, "Better."

She was a remarkable child, Lise thought. Such a wise little owl for five years old. Lise's throat tightened as she busied herself straightening the bed covers. She found Em's Tiny Tears doll tangled in the blanket and settled it on the pillow next to Em. "You have to get better right away," she said. "Do you know why?"

Em looked thoughtful. "So that I can play with my doll?"

Lise laughed. "That too. But I was thinking about the science fair. We're going on a bus all the way to

Los Angeles. It's going to be a wonderful trip, and I want you to come along."

"Los Angeles?" Her eyes widened a little and she reached for the threadbare doll. "Is that like Disneyland?"

"Well, I wouldn't have described it exactly that way, but yes, it's a pretty terrific place."

"Are we going to set up the magnet train and run it for everybody?"

I hope so. Lise nodded.

"Then I'd like to go."

Suddenly Lise had a knot the size of Texas in her stomach. She'd made a commitment to a five-year-old child, that was all. Why did it feel like she'd just promised to part the Red Sea?

LET YOURSELF BE LOVESWEPT BY... SIX BRAND NEW LOVESWEPT ROMANCES!

Because Loveswept romances sell themselves ...we want to send you six (Yes, six!) exciting new novels to enjoy for 15 days — risk free! — without obligation to buy.

Discover how these compelling stories of contemporary romances tug at your heart strings and keep you turning the pages. Meet true-to-life characters you'll fall in love with as their romances blossom. Experience their challenges and triumphs — their laughter, tears and passion.

Let yourself be Loveswept! Join our **at-home reader service!** Each month we'll send you six new Loveswept novels **before they appear in the bookstores.** Take up to **15 days to preview** current selections **risk-free! Keep only those shipments you want.** Each book is yours for only $2.09 plus postage & handling, and sales tax where applicable — **a savings of 41¢ per book** off the cover price.

NO OBLIGATION TO BUY — WITH THIS RISK-FREE OFFER!

YOU GET SIX
ROMANCES RISK FREE...
Plus AN EXCLUSIVE TITLE FREE!

Loveswept Romances

AFFIX
RISK FREE
BOOKS
STAMP
HERE.

Kay Hooper's
**Larger
Than
Life**

This FREE gift
is yours to keep.

MY "NO RISK" GUARANTEE

There's no obligation to buy and the free gift is mine to keep. I may preview each
subsequent shipment for 15 days. If I don't want it, I simply return the books
within 15 days and owe nothing. If I keep them, I will pay just $2.09 per book. I
save $2.50 off the retail price for the 6 books (plus postage and handling, and
sales tax where applicable).

YES! Please send my six Loveswept novels
RISK FREE along with my **FREE GIFT**
described inside the heart! **BR89** 10124

NAME_____

ADDRESS_____ APT_____

CITY_____

STATE_____ ZIP_____

Nine

Stephen sensed the presence of someone in the house even before he heard the soft click of a metal latch bolt. The sound had come from the direction of the living room, and the cabin's front door. He went still, listening intently, his hands poised on the sensor assembly of the device he was calibrating. A floorboard groaned under the intruder's weight, and then the cabin went silent again.

Moving quickly and quietly, Stephen positioned himself against the wall next to the door frame and waited for the door to open. He had an idea who the intruder was. He'd gone into town for supplies that morning, and the stares he attracted weren't just curious, they were hostile. He'd come out of the store to find Buck Thompson leaning against the Land-Rover, a dangerous smirk on his face. That was Buck's first mistake. His second was ignoring Stephen's suggestion that he move.

As a shuffle of footsteps neared, Stephen crouched to pick up a piece of metal tubing. The partially closed door crept open, and a shadow streamed across the floor. Still in a crouch, Stephen swung out the tubing. A muffled scream sounded. The intruder pitched forward in a wild flurry of motion, flailing the air. Only as Stephen collared the prone form and yanked him to his feet did he realize he was dealing with a young boy.

"Who are you?" he demanded.

"I'm Danny Baxter." The boy's face pinched into a grimace, and his pupils shrank with terror. "I wasn't going to steal anything—honest!"

"What are you doing here?" Stephen said, releasing him. He felt a twist of guilt at having roughed up the boy, but given the sensitive nature of his work, he would have tackled anyone coming through that door.

"I—I came to get you," Danny said, urgency in every word. "We need you down at the school."

Adrenaline jolted through Stephen. "Is something wrong? Is it Lise?"

"No—yeah! *Every*thing's wrong! The maglev train won't run and the science fair's next week and you're the only one who can fix it!"

"The maglev train? That's what you came all the way out here for?" Stephen noticed the boy's grimy exhaustion for the first time, and realized he'd probably ridden his bike the entire distance, over twenty miles and most of it uphill. "Does Miss Anderson know you came out here?"

"No, it was my idea. She's been upset the last coupla days. I think she's worried about the train."

Danny's concern was so palpable that Stephen felt himself wavering. He hadn't planned on ever getting within touching distance of Lise Anderson again, but he was carrying a load of guilt about the way he'd left her. Maybe this was his opportunity to repair some of the damage he'd done. Beyond that, how could he justify letting down an entire fifth grade class because he couldn't keep his hands off their ravishing teacher?

The class was in a state of incipient pandemonium by the time Stephen and Danny arrived. Totally unnoticed, Stephen took in the carnival atmosphere for several moments. The kids were busily at work on various parts of the railroad pike, and Lise was completely preoccupied with her own project. She didn't even respond when Danny knelt and tapped her on the shoulder.

Stephen watched her work with awe and some amusement. He'd never seen her in blue jeans before. Beyond that she was on all fours and bent forward on her elbows, investigating the mysteries of a switching mechanism. Several lengths of plastic cording were draped around her neck, and there were instruction sheets scattered all around her.

"Can I help?" Stephen asked.

She froze in place. Moving only her head, she turned to look up at him. It was a moment before she spoke. "Beg your pardon?"

"You look like you're stuck."

If Lise hadn't been stuck before, she was then. The last person in the world she'd expected to see standing in her classroom that afternoon was Stephen Gage. What was he doing there? In addition to the shock buzzing around in her brain, there was one sensible thought. *Get yourself out of this position, Lise.* She rolled up on her haunches and fixed him with what she hoped was a quelling stare.

"Stuck? Whatever made you think that?" she said. "I found a short in the circuit, and I've just fixed it."

By this time the kids had begun to gather around. Lise smiled at them reassuringly. "The problem's solved, gang. Let's get this show on the road. Julie, give it some juice."

"Roger," Julie said, saluting. She threw the switch and jumped back as sparks flew. A puff of smoke rose from the switching mechanism, but the train didn't move. Not a quiver. The class let out a collective groan of dismay.

Lise sprang to her feet. It was everything she could do not to pick the *damn* thing up and chuck it through the window!

"I'd be glad to help," Stephen offered.

"Thank you, but *no*, Mr. Gage," she said, walking to the layout table. "We can manage."

"No, we can't!" the students cried.

Lise stopped midstride and swung around, taking in their anxious expressions. Apparently she had some panic-stricken children on her hands. It hit her then that she'd done very little recently to assuage their fears. In fact, she was probably making things worse with her own anxiety. Yes, she admitted silently, they probably did need Stephen Gage.

"It seems I'm outvoted." She nodded to Stephen rather graciously, she thought, under the circumstances. But there was no mistaking the message in her eyes. *Why did you leave me standing in the rain in my nightgown, Mr. Gage?*

His expression registered regret and frustration. It also registered something even more revealing—a smoldering spark of sexual heat. Whatever had motivated him to throw her out of his van, it hadn't stopped him from wanting her. On the heels of that realization, Lise had a startling flash of insight. Burning deep inside Stephen Gage was a need beyond anything she had ever experienced. It was more than sexual, she knew that instinctively. It was something harsh and faintly sad, and that frightened her a little. What frightened her more was the possibility that he might somehow touch as deep a need in her.

"The train," Julie prompted.

"*Yes*—the train," Lise agreed.

An hour later Stephen had the major problems solved. What was more, he'd managed to involve the children in every aspect of the repair work by asking questions and coaxing the answers out of them as they worked on the model.

He's *good*, Lise thought grudgingly.

"He's brilliant," Julie murmured as though she'd read Lise's mind.

By the time Lise dismissed the class that afternoon, Abraham Lincoln's science lab was a much happier place. Julie seemed to want to linger and stare adoringly at Stephen, but Lise discouraged her with a meaningful glance toward the exit.

"How do you like the new *Star Trek* series, Mr. Gage?" Julie asked on her way out.

Stephen pulled a frown. "*Star trek?*"

Julie looked so shocked that Lise hurried over to escort her out the door. "Stephen obviously doesn't follow television, Julie," she said. "There *are* people who don't sit glued to the tube day and night, believe it or not."

Lise gave Julie a gentle push into the hallway and turned back to Stephen. The girl's words echoed back to them. "But not to know *Star Trek*? You'd have to be from Mars."

"Sorry." Lise met Stephen's blue eyes, and laughed with mild disbelief. "You really haven't heard of *Star Trek*?"

"The television reception is lousy on Mars."

"I'll bet . . ."

As their laughter faded, a pregnant silence crept into the room's atmosphere. With all the unresolved issues between them, Lise was a little stymied about what to do or say next. She drew her lower lip between her teeth. Small talk seemed impossible under the circumstances. "I was just going to lock up and leave," she said.

Moments later they were walking out together, and it was one of the quietest trips of Lise's life. The tension between them grew as they approached the entrance doors. Under other circumstances Lise would have initiated a conversation, but after all, *she* was the one who'd been left standing in the rain, not Stephen. And he'd made no attempt to contact her since.

He stopped her at the bottom of the school's front entrance steps just as they were about to part company. "Could we talk a moment?" he asked.

His eyes were so densely blue, they could have been black. As Lise looked up at him she knew again the pain of being abandoned in the rain. Her father had made her feel inept and clumsy for the best part of her childhood, but she wasn't sure she'd ever felt as deeply inadequate as that night with Stephen.

He shook his head as though he could read in her expression what was going through her mind. "Lise . . . it wasn't you."

She tried to blink away a quick stinging mist. "How could you have done such a thing?"

"It was an emergency—the storm, my equipment—"

He seemed unable, or unwilling, to explain further, but they both knew it wasn't just the storm that had stopped him that night.

As Lise's eyes swept over him her blurred vision created halo effects. Afternoon sunlight fell around them in waves, and for fleeting seconds, a soft white aura enveloped them. His pale hair caught fire. Winter sunshine, Lise thought. She would never again watch it light up the mountains without thinking of him.

"Miss Anderson—"

Lise felt a tugging on the back pocket of her jeans. She turned to see Emily Baxter's stricken face staring up at her.

"Em! What's wrong?" Fear stabbed at Lise's heart. She hadn't seen the little girl since she'd been to the Baxter house with Danny two days before. Was Em worse? Had something terrible happened?

She knelt and drew the child to her, scanning her features. "What is it, sweetheart? Tell me what's wrong?"

"Could the spaceman fix Elizabeth?" Em asked.

That was when Lise noticed the Tiny Tears doll that Em was clutching. One of its arms was hanging by springs and wires. "Is that what's wrong? Is it your doll?"

The child nodded, and Lise was almost light-headed with relief. "How about you, Em?" she asked, checking the child's forehead. "Are you feeling any better?"

Em nodded gravely. "I had waffles for breakfast."

"Waffles? You *must* be better." Actually, the child still looked a little peaked, but she was out of bed and playing and those were both good signs, Lise decided. She had talked with the children's mother and then made arrangements with a neighbor of the Baxter's to keep an eye on the children after school, so she knew Emily had caring supervision now.

"Elizabeth hurt herself," Em said, directing Lise's attention to the doll's sprung arm.

"So I see," Lise agreed. "And you think the spaceman can fix her?"

"I know he can." Her quiet voice was infused with

conviction as she turned her serious gaze upon Stephen and held the doll out. "Here," she said.

Stephen accepted the doll with a solemn nod. "It looks as though Elizabeth has dislocated her shoulder," he said. "Do I have your consent to operate?"

Emily lifted her head in alarm, and then whispered, "Yes."

She watched bravely while he worked, wincing only slightly as he twisted the arm around, made some adjustments to hooks and springs, and then supplied the needed part—a rubber band.

Lise wasn't surprised at Stephen's quick, deft work, but she was intrigued by his occasional glances at Emily. Their eyes would meet for a moment, and Stephen would incline his head slightly, not even a nod. He was reassuring the child, Lise knew, but there was more to it than that. It was as though they understood each other without ever having to say a word.

When Stephen had the doll repaired, he tested its arm with a quick tug, and held it up for Emily to see. She gave a sigh of relief, the most emotion she'd expressed throughout the entire ordeal. Faith *can* move mountains, Lise thought.

"She's something, isn't she?" Lise said a moment later, watching the child wander off.

"She's a mirror to the world," he said quietly. "To its hope, its misery."

Lise turned to him, struck by the depth of his observation. "Yes," she said, "I think you're right . . . that's Em exactly."

His profile was dark against the falling sun, and so unexpectedly lonely, Lise felt her heart begin to pound. A question took shape inside her, and though she didn't fully understand why, she asked it. "Do you have children?"

"No . . . no children."

He said it with the weight of a man who had lost things, vital things, perhaps *everything*. Lise didn't dare to probe further, but she was shaken by the realization, and by her need to understand what was haunting him.

She shivered as they reached her Cordoba moments later. She was sure she hadn't locked the car, but the door handle didn't want to give as she tried it. Stephen's hand was there suddenly, covering hers, forestalling her.

"I wonder if you and I could do something that normal people do?" he said. "Do you think that's possible?"

"Normal people?" She could see her own startled reflection in the car window. And he was there behind her, shadowed in some way that compelled her. His expression was expectant, as though he were as surprised as she was.

"Yes," he said, "I mean things like . . . eating, drinking, dancing? Would you like that? Would you like to have dinner tonight?"

Lise glanced down at his hand, amazed at how much power there was in an unexpected touch. He was asking her out? It made no sense to her given everything that had happened between them, but as she turned the idea over in her mind, it drew her like a magnet. "Yes, I would like that," she said.

Their gaze connected briefly in the window's reflection. Something in the shimmering blue depths of his eyes warned her that he was acting on impulse. And probably against his better judgment.

Aren't we all? she thought.

He came calling for her at six sharp that evening.

Lise opened the door and was pleasantly surprised to see him in fashionably baggy slacks and a stonewashed silk shirt. As though conspiring to enhance the overall effect, the falling sunshine caught the fringes of his hair and turned it to firelight.

He cleans up well, Lise thought ironically. Julie's "babe" reference had been a masterpiece of understatement. Stephen Gage was alarmingly masculine and sexy.

He took in her powder-blue halter-top dress with a slow, appreciative sweep of his eyes. "You look beautiful." Handing her a boxed corsage of creamy white gardenias, he added, "I hope these are all right."

"Oh, my gosh—" her voice softened to whispered laughter, "—are you taking me to the prom?"

"Prom?"

His puzzlement made her shake her head in disbelief. "You don't know what a *prom* is?"

"Oh, I know what it is. I just don't know why you'd want to go to one."

"*Every* high-school girl wants to go to the prom." Her throat tightened as she met his questioning gaze. Wistfully she admitted, "I was never asked."

His eyes flared with tenderness as he took the corsage from her hand. "Come here, Miss Anderson," he said, "and let me pin this on you."

The rich scent of gardenias drenched Lise's front porch as Stephen slipped his fingers under the strap of her sundress. Lise knew his intention was to use his own hand to protect her from the pin. But knowing did very little to soften the impact of his nearness, or the sudden warmth of his skin on hers.

He was affected by it too. She could hear his breathing deepen and feel the hesitation in his hands as he positioned the flower on the halter strap. It was inevitable that his hands would brush her breast as he began to work with the pin.

"Sorry," he murmured, glancing up at her. The blue of his eyes nearly drowning her in expectation.

The pin resisted as he eased it into the corsage. And then his wrist nudged her cleavage, freckles and all! Lise's stomach clutched. She could feel the jut of his wristbone, the feather tickle of golden hair.

"Don't breathe," he said, trying another angle. He probed gently here and there, applying more force as he found the right spot. There was a moment of pressure before the resistance gave way and the needle penetrated. Lise let go of the breath she was holding, and a liquid sensation rippled down her thighs. She was weak in the knees by the time he slipped his fingers out from under the strap.

He stepped back and looked her over. "It's official,"

he said, his voice husky with male appreciation. "You're my date for the prom."

Lise glanced from the delicate flowers to his burnished handsomeness. If she was slightly rattled by the incident, she was even more unprepared for the thoughts that were creeping into her consciousness. She didn't want to go to a prom, not really. She didn't want to go *anywhere* with this golden lion of a man except straight to the nearest bedroom, which in this case, was her own. He had once looked as though he wanted to eat her alive. If she'd seen even a hint of that same thrilling hunger now, she would have abandoned propriety altogether and offered herself up for his pleasure.

"Ready to go?" he said.

She nodded.

Moments later they were in his Land-Rover and driving off in search of a "prom." Lise was acutely uncomfortable at the ogling they got from the local citizenry as they cruised through town. At one point Bernice Davenport ambled up to the Rover when they were stopped at a crosswalk, wanting to know what they were up to. "Just a quick bite to eat," Lise assured her.

"What a good idea, dear," Bernice said, smiling at Stephen. "Adios," she called out as she hurried off.

No doubt to spread the news, Lise thought, sighing. "Let's find a prom *outside* of town," she suggested to Stephen.

They finally settled for a roadhouse on the county highway. It wasn't quite what Lise had in mind, but the golden oldies on the jukebox and the stacked high, juicy hamburgers took her back to her adolescent years as effectively as if they'd gone to a dance in the high-school gym.

Watching Stephen tear into his double-decker hamburger and fries, Lise had to suppress a chuckle. He'd unbuttoned his shirt collar and rolled up his sleeves, and he looked about as down-home and middle-American as it was possible to be. She should snap a picture for Julie, she thought. This would make a believer out of her.

They were lingering over after-dinner coffee and casual conversation when Stephen brought up the incident that had been hovering in the background of Lise's thoughts.

"That night on the mountain," he said. "I'm sorry about what happened, Lise. It wasn't just the storm as you've probably already guessed."

"I guessed." She also sensed that whatever the problem was, he'd been living with it for a very long time. Distress lay deep in his eyes. From the rugged strength of his features, she might have estimated his age as somewhere in the midthirties, but tonight she wasn't sure. He had the weary wisdom of someone who had lived through several lifetimes and seen more than his share of tragedy.

"It's all right," she said. "You don't have to talk about it if you'd rather not."

Stephen curled both hands around his empty coffee mug. *If I'd rather not*, he thought, staring at the rings and water marks that scarred the surface of their wooden table. He'd never revealed the truth of his past to anyone, and under any other circumstances, he wouldn't have considered doing so then. But he knew she would never understand otherwise. She might be a wizard at life in general, but she was still virginal and uncertain when it came to men. If he didn't make an attempt to explain—*if he didn't tell her the truth about what he'd done*—she would always think it was her fault they hadn't made love.

"If I don't talk about it now," he said, exhaling heavily, "I never will." He looked up at last. "I'll give it a shot if you're game."

"Of course—*please*." She concentrated on her own half-full coffee cup as though she could sense his discomfort.

"I was married once, right out of college," he began. "Actually, it was the year I was to graduate . . . and she was pregnant."

Lise recoiled at the last word. Her first reaction was

simple disbelief. She couldn't fathom the idea that he'd been married. It was too normal. It gave him a past. It made him a man. But what sank in as she glanced at him was a deeper realization, a deeper fear. He *was* a man. He was going to tell her about another woman in his life, perhaps his first love. She wasn't sure she wanted to hear that story—*she was afraid to hear it*—but there was so much anger and self-condemnation trapped in his voice, so much harsh regret, she had no choice.

"Stephen," she said, "that happens."

"No—this was different. I made it happen. She was the dean's daughter. I didn't just want her, I was obsessed. In my mind, making love to her was the way to lay claim, and I didn't give up until she—" He broke off, exhaling. "I didn't force her, unless you call mindless, relentless pursuit, force."

Lise couldn't summon a response. Her feelings were too divided. She felt compassion for his obvious suffering, and anguished surprise at her own.

He pushed the coffee cup away and went on. "She'd never been with another man either. I wanted to be the first—"

The self-disgust in his voice was explosive. But Lise wasn't reacting to that. She'd barely heard it. A searing pain nearly closed off her throat. *He'd wanted to be the first.*

"You must have been in love with her," she said, wishing to Heaven she didn't need to know. "Deeply in love."

It took him a long time to answer. "If I was in love," he said, "it was for all the wrong reasons. No, I didn't love her. Not the way I should have, and that makes it all the more tragic."

"Tragic? Because the marriage failed?"

"It didn't fail. She died in childbirth. They both died."

"The baby . . . ?"

He turned away, and Lise couldn't say anything for a moment.

"Stephen . . . *I'm sorry.*"

His voice was flattened and toneless, as permanently scarred as the wooden tabletop. "Don't be sorry for me. I don't deserve it. Be sorry for them."

Several horror-filled seconds flashed by. Lise's thoughts were reeling. She didn't know what to think or how to feel. She didn't know how to comfort him. His revelations were shocking, and yet so much of what had happened made sense now, the ravages of time, the shadowed pain, and especially the way he'd reacted on the mountain.

A popular song was playing in the background, a poignant echo of Lise's jumbled feelings. Stephen's shoulders were stiffened, his posture forbidding. She wanted to break through the barrier he'd raised, but she was genuinely afraid of his reaction. She reached to touch his arm and jerked back as he turned.

"Maybe we ought to go," he said abruptly. "I think the prom's over." He dug in his pocket and threw some money down on the table.

Lise tried to think how to stop him as he pushed back the chair and stood. "How could the prom be over?" she said. "We didn't even dance."

"Dance?"

"The waltz, the fox-trot, Fred and Ginger used to do it."

"You want to waltz?" He stared at her incredulously and his voice dropped to something low and cold. "Your timing stinks, you know that?"

"I don't want this evening to be over yet, that's all I know." She fought back an upsurge of emotion. She was revealing more of herself than she wanted to, but she knew if things ended this way, she would never see him again. "I want the chance to get to know you better, Stephen."

He regarded her with disbelief and a harsh sound of anger. "Why, Lise?" Flattening his palm on the table, he leaned toward her. "It's hardly worth your time or trouble. I'll only be here a few more days. There's no future for us."

"I don't remember asking for a future." She met his

hard blue eyes, determined to deflect their cruelness. It was himself he wanted to hurt.

"Stephen, please." She laid her hand on his sleeve and froze. The cold contempt in his eyes brought the warmth of his body into sharp contrast. He didn't want her touching him. He didn't want her anywhere near him.

"Maybe you're right," she said, profoundly saddened. "The prom *is* over."

What A Fool Believes was playing on the jukebox as Lise forced back her chair and rose, pushing past Stephen. She hesitated a moment as the seventies ballad brought back memories of an adolescence that was lonely and confused. It brought back a young girl's longings, and a heart full of dreams that had gone begging. She glanced at the half-dozen couples on the dance floor and their swaying bliss made her even sadder.

"I'll be outside," she said, starting for the door. She hadn't gone two steps before Stephen caught up with her.

"Lise . . . *don't leave.*"

His voice was a harsh, riveting whisper. Before Lise could react, he'd taken hold of her shoulders and brought her around to face him. His hands were taut. His darkened eyes held anger, sadness, an apology.

"What are you doing?" she asked as he took her by the hand.

"I don't know, Lise. I don't know what the hell I'm doing anymore. You wanted to dance, didn't you?"

He led her onto the sawdust-strewn dance floor and into his arms. She could feel the tenseness in him as he fitted his hand to the small of her back. It was as though he'd raised an invisible barrier, and yet Lise knew he wanted to pull her close. She could feel it in the depth of his breathing, and in the muscular tension he gave off. He needed to be close to a woman. Badly. But he wouldn't let himself.

"It's been a long time," she said, meaning the dancing.

"A very long time," he said.

There were the inevitable moments of awkwardness as they began to move. It seemed to take forever until they found a compatible dance step, and then gradually the music began to work its sad, sweet magic. Almost imperceptibly the slow throb of the ballad insinuated itself into their stiff movements. They began to sway a little. They drew a fraction closer. An irresistible rhythm was taking hold.

A current of electricity sprinkled Lise's palm as she ran her hand along the stonewashed silk of his shirt. She'd never been in his arms before, at least not like this, with such carefully calculated distance between them. The fact that their bodies weren't touching as they moved only heightened her awareness of him. Her imagination was vividly supplying the missing details. It was telling her how it would feel to be pressed up against every solid inch of him.

Their thighs brushed, and he swore softly. "It's been *too* long," he said, pulling her closer.

She yielded instinctively, flowing into his heat. He gripped her hand tighter, and as his arm locked around her, she softened against his hard contours like seawater eddying against rocks. She heard an exhalation, and realized it was his—a mesmerizingly throaty sound that was lost in the swell of the music. It's been *forever*, she thought. *I've never danced like this before.*

The musculature of his shoulder rippled under her hand, drawing her awareness to that part of his body. Gradually she realized that her fingertips were nestled in the glossy thickness of his hair. I don't believe this, she thought. *I'm at the prom . . . with the boy of my dreams.* As the scent of gardenias eddied around them, she swallowed a bittersweet sigh. She felt as though every sweet yearning she'd ever had was being realized in this gentle moment of reckoning.

"Thank you," she said.

"For what?" His lips were against her temple.

"For this."

He pulled her closer, and she could feel the need shaking through him. She'd never, ever had a man respond to her as he did. He needed caring for, he needed holding so desperately it made her ache. She laid her head against his cheek and whispered five soft words. "I *am* sorry for you."

Ten

"Miss Anderson, are you picking daisies?"

"Hmmm?" Lise glanced around the railroad pike where she and her class had spent the morning putting the finishing touches on their futuristic vision of Los Angeles. Em Baxter had asked the question, Lise realized. The five-year-old's forehead was knitted into a thoughtful frown.

"Picking daisies, Em?"

The child hunched her small shoulders. "My mom always asks me that when I'm daydreaming. You keep staring out the window, is all."

"I do?" Lise considered the front window, completely unaware that she'd been staring anywhere.

"And you just glued another dogwood tree to the *freeway!*" Danny Baxter yelped. "Look!"

Everyone did look, including Lise. Two trees appeared to have taken root square in the middle of Interstate 5.

Lise flushed with soft laughter and rolled her eyes, which her students seemed to think was hilarious.

Julie flashed a wicked grin from the other side of the pike. "And just what did *you* do last night, Miss Anderson?" she said. "You were seen cruising around in Flash Gordon's Land-Rover!"

A low gasp ricochetted through the room.

The warmth in Lise's cheeks deepened. Normally she

wouldn't have dreamed of discussing the details of her personal life with her students, but she simply couldn't hold it in. "I went to a prom," she said.

"With the *spaceman*?" Em Baxter blinked in disbelief.

"Yes, Em—and his name is Mr. Gage." Lise touched her shoulder lingeringly, remembering the corsage. "He even brought me gardenias."

By that time the entire class was staring at Lise as though she'd gone crazy, but she hardly minded. She was remembering how she and Stephen had slow danced until midnight to steamy pop ballads of the past, songs full of sexual longing and unrequited love. She was remembering the wild thrill of his arms around her—and the sweetest moments of all—when the music stopped and they continued to sway on the dance floor, unwilling to let go of the moment, or the music, or each other.

She was remembering the ache in her throat when he told her what a miracle of life she was. And she was reliving a good-night kiss on her front porch. A kiss of such urgent tenderness and passion that it left her reeling. It had been the most wonderful night of her life . . .

"Miss Anderson!"

The raspy male voice catapulted Lise back to the present. She glanced at her students' startled faces as someone began pounding frantically on the classroom door.

"Miss Anderson!"

Lise jerked around as the school's janitor, a thin, balding man in his fifties, burst into the room.

"What is it, Earl?" she asked.

"It's them museum statues—" Earl yanked a blue handkerchief out of his hip pocket and wiped his forehead with it. "Buck Thompson claims he found one of 'em buried out on the Cooper property. He says it's proof positive the spaceman took 'em."

Lise's reaction was immediate and angry. "If Buck Thompson found a statue on the Cooper property," she muttered, "it's probably because *he* buried it there." It hadn't occurred to her before that Buck might have been the one to take the statues, but it made perfect sense now that she thought about it. What better way to cast suspicion on Stephen?

Lise held up a hand and turned to her class, calming their excited buzzing. "It's all right, gang. I'll get to the bottom of this. Julie, take over for me," she said, motioning Earl toward the door.

Earl swung around the minute they were out in the hallway. "That ain't all, Miss Anderson," he said, his voice hushed. "I didn't want to say it in front of the kids, but the Davenport sisters are missing."

"Missing?"

"Yes, ma'am. They ain't been seen since yesterday, and nobody knows where they went. Buck and the guys at Frank's station are saying *he* had something to do with it—"

"Wait a minute, Earl," Lise cut in. "I saw Bernice last night. She was on her way home from the library. Did you check their house?"

"Yes, ma'am. Norbert Potts stopped by there this morning when Miss Bernice didn't show up for work. He tried calling first, but nobody answered the phone."

The Davenport sisters missing? Lise was trying to remember what Bernice had said last night. Nothing unusual except, *Adios*? Was that the word she'd used? "*Adios . . .*" Lise said, thinking aloud, searching for a connection. "Earl! Maybe they went on that Mexican cruise they're always talking about!"

Earl wrinkled his nose. "Bernice Davenport would never traipse off to Mexico and leave the public library high and dry. Why, she's been our foremost reference person for thirty-five years. And she's never taken a day off in all that time."

Earl was right, of course. Neither of the Davenport sisters would do anything so irresponsible. "Well, I'm sure they're all right."

"More'n I can say for your outer-space friend once Frank's boys get hold of him," Earl said ominously.

"What do you mean?"

"There's a bunch of 'em headed for the hills about

fifteen minutes ago. I s'pect they're going to rough him up pretty good if they don't get some answers."

Lise's heart jolted. "But that's ridiculous. Stephen didn't do anything!" She touched the janitor's arm, staying him while she mobilized her thoughts. "Earl, I need your help. Tell Julie to take over the class until I get back. Then, run down to city hall and tell Billy Cornmesser to get out to Stephen's cabin as fast as he can. Tell him I'm on my way there now."

"You oughten to go all by yourself!" Earl called after Lise as she sprinted down the hallway. "Billy ain't going to be no help, Miss Anderson! He's down at the courthouse testifying on some traffic thing."

Lise shook her head and kept running. She would have to handle it on her own then. There wasn't time to find anyone else, especially an ally who could be expected to take Stephen's side against Buck Thompson and his friends. Perhaps she should have sought Buck out herself and tried to talk some sense into him. Their infrequent dates had been years ago, but Buck had never stopped asking her out. And there was something distinctly territorial about him—a cocky swagger that warned other men off. Lord, if she'd contributed to this nightmare, even unknowingly, she would never forgive herself.

Lise drove the deserted road to the hills with a recklessness fueled by fear. Violent images flashed through her mind, impelling her. She desperately wanted to believe the men wouldn't hurt Stephen, but in her heart she knew they were capable of anything. Buck saw Stephen as a rival, and he was obviously willing to go to any lengths to turn the town against him. With the Davenport sisters missing and the statue conveniently turning up, he'd probably whipped his cohorts into a frenzy of vigilantism.

The thought of anything happening to Stephen filled Lise with dread. She had promised herself years ago that she would never do what her mother had done— let a man become the center of her world, let him become everything in her life. And yet in a few short days Stephen had become the center of her world. It felt as though he *were* everything.

Dust enveloped the jolting Cordoba as she sped down the rutted dirt access road. The cabin came into view, and as the brown haze cleared, she was a horrified witness to the mayhem she'd imagined earlier. It was a full-scale assault. A half-dozen men had descended upon Stephen, most of them fighting to restrain him as he twisted and whirled.

A small, wiry man clung to Stephen's back like a monkey. Another man leapt at him, and another, all of them piling on. Stephen jackknifed forward, throwing two of them over his head. They rushed him again, flying at him, dragging him down. He fought furiously, but he was hopelessly outnumbered. Arms locked around his throat, torso, and legs, anchoring him. His arms were pinned back.

Lise pulled the car to a stop, bursting out just as Buck Thompson drove his fist savagely into Stephen's midsection. Stephen reared up with a violent sound, and it took all six men to hold him down. Buck lashed out again, landing blow after brutal blow. Stephen convulsed and doubled over.

"Buck! All of you!" Lise screamed. "Let him go! *Now*!!"

Heads turned and Buck grinned insolently. "I ain't gonna *hurt* your boyfriend, Lise. I'm gonna annihilate him!"

He whirled and jammed an elbow into Stephen's ribs.

Lise heard the sickening crack of bone and sinew as Buck followed the elbow with a fist. *"No!"* she cried as Stephen sagged to his knees. *They were going to kill him!*

She spotted what looked like a wooden rifle butt sticking out of the pickup truck's bed. A gun? It was her only chance! Seconds later she had Buck Thompson's ugly face fixed in the sites of a hunting rifle. The rifle made an explosive sound as she cocked it.

"Stop!" she shouted. "Stop or I'll *shoot*!"

Several of the men whirled in Lise's direction and

froze. The rest halted where they stood. "Let him go," she said.

Stephen slumped to the ground as the men released him. Fear stabbed at Lise as she tried to determine how badly he was hurt. He lay prone, bruised and smeared with blood, perhaps even unconscious.

Bastards, she thought, jerking the gun barrel at Buck. "Get out of here! All of you!"

"Hell, *Ms.* Anderson," Buck said, a sneer twisting his lips. "You're not going to use that thing."

"Get back!" Lise cried as he started toward her. Her finger froze on the trigger, and panic slammed through her body.

A savage roar erupted from behind Buck. Stephen wrenched to his feet and flung himself at the man's back, flattening him with a shoulder slam. As the two men sprawled on the ground, rolling and thrashing, the others crowded around. Within seconds it was another vicious melee. The men who weren't brawling shouted and jeered, aiming kicks and blows at Stephen.

Lise swung the rifle barrel in the air and squeezed off a round. The report was explosive. A hard jolt of pain knocked her backward as the gun kicked violently.

Trembling, she caught her balance and leveled the barrel at the hovering men. "I never thought I could shoot a man," she said, her voice strangled with emotion. "*Dammit*—don't make me have to find out!"

Tears stung Lise's eyes as she stood next to the bed, staring down at Stephen's bloodied features. Semiconscious, he murmured something incoherently and swung out an arm. He was still fighting off his attackers, she realized.

"They're gone," she said, knowing he couldn't hear her. She glanced out the window, shaking uncontrollably in the aftermath of the violence. They *were* gone, thankfully. She'd had to put a bullet in the dirt at Buck Thompson's feet to convince Frank's boys that she meant business. But once she'd done that, they seemed willing enough to listen to her lecture on mind-less vigilante violence. Afterward she'd had Harry Barnes carry Stephen into the house—and sent them all packing.

Now that she was alone, she had to get hold of her-self and treat Stephen's wounds. She brought an icy fist to her chest, telling herself it was a delayed reac-tion. She'd never felt as shaken and helpless, and something in her heart ached so fiercely, she couldn't move. *I'm sorry,* she thought. *I'm sorry if I was the cause of any of this.*

Moments later she was sitting beside him, gingerly washing the blood from his face and neck. Only one laceration on his forehead required bandaging. The rest were scratches and minor cuts. Most of the blows had been to his body, which meant she was going to have to open his shirt.

She'd worked all the buttons free and spread open the torn chambray material before she realized how savagely they'd beaten him. *"Oh, my Lord,"* she whis-pered, afraid even to touch the swollen crimson welts and violent purple bruises.

A cut below his ribs was oozing freely and she forced herself to set about cleaning it. She'd never been squeamish about blood or taking care of the sick, but with him it was different. He was bleeding because of her, and she couldn't stand the thought of causing him any more pain.

He moaned as she applied a large adhesive bandage to the cut, and her heart clutched painfully. "Ste-phen?" she said, touching his face. "Are you all right? Can you hear me?"

His head was twisted away from her, and the spiky growth of his beard abraded her palm as she brought his face around. His eyes were closed, his jaw slack, and the utter stillness of him filled her with dread. It was as though some vital energy had drained out of him. The blue desolation she'd seen in his eyes, the wildness of deep space, had defined him. Without it, he didn't seem to exist.

None of that, Lise, she told herself, holding his face in her shaking hands. *Stop it now. You're scaring yourself.* He was simply unconscious, and if he didn't come to soon, she would have to call a doctor. He wouldn't want that, she knew, but she had no other recourse.

Lise knew first aid. She'd had to check unconscious students more than once for signs of a concussion, and she was relieved to find Stephen's pupils equal in size and responsive to light. Once she'd assured herself that his breathing and heart rate were normal, she began cleaning the rest of his wounds.

It wasn't until she was washing her hands in the bathroom that she noticed the crimson stain on the side of her skirt. He was still bleeding somewhere! She returned to the bedroom, searching him for the wound. His pants' leg was twisted around, and as she straightened it, she saw that the knee of his jeans was ripped out.

It was a nasty cut. Lise dabbed at the wound through the torn denim, aware that she was only delaying the inevitable. Not only couldn't she stem the blood flow, but the jeans were smeared with dirt, and the risk of infection was enormous.

She rose from the bed with a heavy sigh and stared down at him. History repeats itself, she thought, bemused. She and Stephen Gage seemed fated to remove each other's clothing. He had the easier time of it, she decided, wondering how in the world she was going to get denim jeans off a massively built, unconscious man.

She refused to let herself think about anything other than his injured knee as she worked open the button of his fly. Unfortunately for her good intentions, it was inevitable that her rigid fingers would come into contact with the corded muscle of his abdomen and the golden hair that flared from his beltline.

Thoughts crept into her mind that she didn't want to deal with. Totally inappropriate thoughts about how different the male body was from the female . . . how hard and unyielding the muscles, how wedged and narrow the hips. *Stop it, Lise.*

She sat back to steady her breathing, and let her gaze sweep over him. A crucial mistake. Perhaps she could have dealt with him part by part, but taken as a whole, he was a devastatingly beautiful man, even with the injuries. With his shirt flung open and his pants undone, he was a riveting mix of raw sensuality and vulnerability.

Her hand was shaking as she gripped the zipper's pull tab and drew down the slide. Golden hair caressed her fingers all the way to the metal bottom stop. *"I knew it,"* she whispered, closing her eyes. He wasn't wearing a stitch under the pants!

She kept her eyes shut as she gripped the jean's waistband and began to tug the pants down. Just do it, Lise, she told herself, trying not to be aware of what she was touching. With some awkwardness, she managed to get the pants free of his hips and down to his thighs. Upon reaching his injured knee, she opened her eyes to be sure she wasn't doing any more damage.

The only major snag was his feet. She'd forgotten to remove his shoes. They were an odd kind of sandal made of a woven leatherlike material she'd never seen before. She slipped them off, scanning them for a brand name, but there wasn't one to be found—and her interest in such things vanished as she looked up.

Her breathing deepened as she stared at him. Everything seemed to be slowing down, even her thoughts. Opened shirt notwithstanding, he *was* naked. Despite all his injuries, despite everything he'd been through, Lise's first—her only—thought was that. Stephen Gage lay naked before her eyes. She was shocked at herself for gaping. She was even vaguely ashamed under the circumstances, but the reason was obvious. She'd never witnessed living, breathing male nudity before. He was the first.

As it dawned on her that she had unfinished business with his naked male body, her heart did a somersault. And then it slammed up against her chest wall as though it wanted out.

Hopelessly awkward, she began to remove the crusted dirt and blood from his knee injury. She could hardly get her hands under control, and she knew very well what was distracting her. As her eyes kept drifting to *that* part of him, she finally took some remedial action. Dragging up a section of the chenille bedspread, she draped it over his midsection.

Another injury caught her eye as she covered him. There was a jagged rent where his hipbone sloped into his pelvis. *That* one would have to wait, she decided. Perhaps forever.

But moments later, as she finished with his knee, her thoughts were drawn again to the pelvic injury. There had been something strange about it. She touched the chenille tentatively, and finally drew it aside.

The wound was jagged and bluish, but as she looked closer she saw that it wasn't a laceration. It was some sort of mark, not a tattoo exactly, but similar. Lightning, she realized with a start. She was staring at twin bolts of lightning! They were flawlessly drawn and perfectly symmetrical. Curious, Lise brushed a finger over one of the blue streaks and felt its raised outline.

Stephen stirred as she touched him, and Lise looked up. She couldn't tell whether he was responding to her touch—or to where she'd touched him. She pressed the mark again, and he moaned out a word she didn't understand.

"Stephen?" She moved up to him, touching his face. His eyes drifted open and after a moment he seemed to focus in on her. "Are you all right?" she asked.

Again he said a word she didn't understand, and she tried to follow the movement of his lips. "Runes? Is that what you said, Stephen? What does it mean?"

"Yes, runes. Get them, Lise. Get the stones."

"I don't understand."

"They're in my knapsack . . . get them."

Lise rifled through his knapsack, digging into one zipper pouch after another until she found a small metal box. Inside were two smooth black stones, oblong in shape, and about the size of walnuts. As she tipped the box and emptied them into her palm, she had the oddest sensation of movement. The stones seemed to come alive in her hands, and though she couldn't actually see them moving, she could feel their inner vibrance and energy.

"Hold them in your hands, Lise," Stephen said. "They respond to body heat."

Lise cupped the stones tightly and watched with silent amazement as a misty bluish light began to seep through the cracks in her fingers. It reminded her of the quarry lights except that it was a deeper blue, and even more luminous. "Stephen, what are they?"

"Lodestones," he said, his voice gaining strength, "a form of magnetized rock . . . with healing properties."

She could feel their warmth and energy building within the confinement of her hands. "Healing properties?"

He tried to sit up and his jaw clenched in pain. "Come here, Lise. Hold them so that the light falls through your fingers."

Lise moved to the bed, opening her hands slightly to let the radiant energy glow through. She sat next to him, hesitating only a moment before her movements became instinctive. Bathing him in the strange blue light, she started at his breastbone and moved her cupped hands in ever-widening circles. The stones seemed to shudder in her hands. Lise could feel the power they held . . . and yet nothing appeared to be happening as she swirled the intense blue beam over his body. There was no visible effect on his wounds.

Gradually she began to sense that the stones were controlling her movements, pulling her hands with the flow of light. As the cool blue fire circled his body hypnotically, she could feel herself being drawn into its orbit. . . .

She came to with a start, having no idea how much time had passed. As her thoughts cleared she realized she'd forgotten all about his injuries. A sense of wonderment crept over her as she scanned his body. Was it a trick of the light? Was she imagining the effect?

The cuts seemed to be drawing up, the bruises diminishing.

Stephen's breathing deepened, and his taut stomach muscles released some of their tension. Lise pulled back, her heart quickening. Something *was* happening.

"Don't be afraid," he said. "Let the light flow off your fingertips . . . touch me."

She had no idea what he meant until he showed her how to hold the stones loosely in the mouth of her hand, exactly as though she were wielding a pencil. Blue light streamed off her fingertips as she moved them over his body.

The natural light was fading as the sun dropped behind the hills outside, and in the room's deepening shadows, the stones' silvery blue phosphorescence seemed to be the only illumination. It was an eerily beautiful effect that made Lise realize for the first time the strangeness of the situation.

Outside the cabin a bird cried, haunting and forlorn.

Stephen lay stretched out beneath her, his eyes closed as though all of his energy were being directed to the healing rays. His near nakedness drew her attention to the marks on his pelvis, and questions began to gather, overriding all her other thoughts. Who was this man with lightning bolts on his body? Where had he come from? What was he doing here?

At the roadhouse last night, he'd shared his past, and she had listened and ached for him. She'd known heartbreak and loneliness too. She'd always expected to spend the rest of her life alone, but in the course of one evening, she'd come to think of him as a kindred spirit. The depth of his pain, the brutality of his self-imposed isolation had moved her. It had opened her heart. When they'd danced together, she'd allowed herself the sweet burn of dreams, of hope. There'd been a crazy sense of certainty, of knowing . . .

Now she was certain of nothing. His body had been brutalized. He was vulnerable, staggeringly beautiful even in his wounded state. But he wasn't a kindred spirit. He wasn't the man she'd been with last night.

She let her eyes sweep over him, and the questions in her mind stormed unanswered for several seconds. A swatch of bedspread covered the most virile part of his body, and despite her resistance, she found her gaze drawn back to it again and again. Her hand pulsed with the stones' energy, and the light streamed through her fingers, spilling recklessly over his torso, as drawn to that part of him as her eyes.

The stones' power was increasing, she realized, and the more she resisted, the more restless they became in her hands. She felt like a child, transfixed by dread, by excitement as the flow of blue pulled her along in its wake. Something was happening to her, and it wasn't just a physical sensation. It was affecting her reasoning, her will. She turned her hand and opened it, held by the stones' soft brilliance.

The marks on his body flashed in her psyche, and suddenly she knew what she had to do. The impulse that took hold of her was as powerful as anything she'd ever felt. Her heart burned with a crazy, racing heat as she curled her hand over the stones and reached toward his groin.

Her fingertips seemed to create sparks as she touched him. She traced the lightning bolts, mesmerized, and then, unable to stop herself, she let her fingers drift along his hipbone and down the muscled length of his thigh.

The constriction in her belly cinched tighter as she realized where her imagination was taking her, *where her hands were taking her.* A strange liquid heaviness invaded her loins and rippled down her legs. It was a beautiful, weakening feeling. The inside of her thighs began to ache softly as though she'd strained muscles there.

It hit her then. The realizations came at her one by one, like the buffeting force of ocean waves.

She wanted to make love with him.

Now . . .

Here . . .

She wanted to be transported . . . taken.

No! That was impossible. He was injured.

But she did. She wanted to make love. Here. In all the thrilling, strange darkness that surrounded them. Now. She wanted the wildness, the loneliness locked inside him. She wanted the fiery rage, the shadowy pain, she wanted it all.

"Stephen, I—"

Stephen lay unmoving as her fingers jerked to a halt. He'd been aware for several seconds of the rising tension in her touch, the rigidity in her movements. In the quiet of his mind, he understood her conflict. She was confused and frightened by what was happening to her, and in her panic, she wanted desperately to believe that it was some supernatural force driving her. But it wasn't the stones' power that frightened Lise Anderson. It was her own. She was in need. Her body was speaking its will, but she had denied her natural urges for so long, they'd become the enemy.

"Touch me, Lise . . ."

A sweet, hurt sound came out of her, and her fingers began to move jerkily. The universe had a rhythm that played itself out in anyone who would listen, anyone who could hear it. That rhythm was beating in her now, but she was resisting its call.

Sweet resistance. He could feel the beginnings of it in his own body too. Deep muscles were stirring, and his limbs felt weighted. There was a languid density in his tissues that came of gathering blood and rising body heat. His physical being was urging him not to resist.

It was a battle he couldn't win. And yet, like her, he didn't want to give himself over to it. He didn't want to lose his will to the tyranny of desire. It was beautiful and terrifying, that primal call to power. There was a searing tenderness at the center of his being, and with every trembling stroke of her fingers, she sent a laser of energy to that tender, bruised place.

The rhythm was calling him too.

The hard ache of mating was in him.

Eleven

The light glowing off Lise's fingertips illuminated the corded muscle of Stephen's thigh and turned his body hair to rippling silver. Though she could sense the steely tension mounting inside him, she wasn't consciously aware of the changes taking place in his body. She was too much in awe of her own trembling responses.

"Put the stones aside, Lise," he said. "Set them on the dresser and come here."

His voice came as a shock to her senses. Its hoarseness spoke of male need. Its low jolt of command compelled her to do as he asked.

It wasn't a question of resisting him. She couldn't have even if she'd wanted to. The attraction was fundamental. She was a flower bending to light, air rushing into a vacuum.

She deposited the stones on the dresser top and turned back to him, her hands still alive with vibrant energy. A cool glow spilled from the dresser top, cloaking her in blue mists.

"Finish it, Lise," he said huskily. "Finish the healing—*with your hands.*"

Fear and excitement mingled in the pit of Lise's stomach. The heady mix flashed through her, stealing her breath and her strength. She hardly knew what she was doing as she walked to the bed and sat next to him. Her hands moved automatically to the power of his chest. Brawn, she thought absently, following the whorls of silver that defined his pectorals. Wasn't that what they called the dense, striated muscle she was touching?

The silver drifted toward his groin, and as she followed its path over his abdomen, she was aware of bruises and tender knots beneath her fingers. The hellishness of his injuries abraded her skin, reminding her of the beating he'd taken.

And then she touched something familiar, the jagged lightning streaks that were burned into his hipbone. She closed her eyes as her fingers connected next with the bedspread. That was as far as she could go. He was aroused!

"Take it off, Lise. Remove the blanket."

Her head snapped up in surprise. "I *can't*," she said. "I've never—"

The room's blue glow turned him into something harsh and desolate, something to be feared. The feral hunger was in his eyes, the wild, terrifying beauty she'd seen before. She knew who he was. And why she was frightened. He was the man who had ravished her senses in the supply room, the man who'd blindfolded and abducted her.

"Take the blanket off me," he said.

She shook her head, but the tumult inside her bled all the strength out of her refusal. His need to control was far more powerful than hers to resist. For the first time she began to believe that whatever was driving him might not be human. Fear clutched at her throat, and deep inside, she felt an explosion of wild, anguished excitement.

"Do it, Lise—"

"*No*—"

"You want to, dammit. *Do* it."

"You don't know what I want!"

But he did. They both knew what she wanted.

Her hands shook uncontrollably as she lifted the chenille material and threw it aside. She drew in a sharp breath as she witnessed the graphic evidence of his arousal. Needles of heat pierced her throat and jawline, turning her skin scarlet. And yet, despite her body's profound agitation, or perhaps because of it, her reaction was anger. In that moment, the rigid male flesh seemed to symbolize everything that was prideful and arrogant and domineering about the masculine sex. *Everything she had fought to escape.*

A soft cry of indignation flared through her. "Why are you making me do this?" she said, turning to him.

He raised himself up, caught her by the wrist and pulled her to him. "Why are you pretending you don't *want* this?"

Tears burned her eyes and choked her throat. "How am I supposed to know what I want? I've never done any of this before!"

"Then it's time, dammit. It's time you did it *all.*"

She pulled away from him, stung and breathless. "And I suppose I should do it all with *you*? Is that what you had in mind?"

"That's exactly what I had in mind." His eyes grazed her body, lingering on her breasts with a long, slow burn. "Are you going to take your clothes off, Lise? Or am I?"

"You're outrageous—"

He caught hold of her wrist again, and she twisted away, whirling off the bed. Anger lent her grace of movement. She was fluid, a red streak of fury as she reached the dresser and gripped it to calm herself. Blue light glowed over her, its effect strangely soothing as she drew in a deep, shaking breath. It was several moments before she could collect herself enough to speak.

"My father was a domineering bastard," she said at last, her back to Stephen. "He made my mother's life hell, and he would have destroyed mine too—" She broke off with a strangled sound and turned "—but I wouldn't let him do that to me. And I won't let you either."

He stared at her for a long time, but his gaze had turned inward, burning with an emotion that frightened Lise as much as the hunger had. It was anger and self-loathing. "No, don't let me do that to you, Lise," he said, sinking back to the bed. "Don't let me near you."

Lise was held by a dawning awareness as she observed him. The ravages of his body were nothing compared to the devastation inside. When he lashed out at her, when he was cruel, it was himself he wanted to hurt. He'd never forgiven himself for the death of his wife and child. He'd sought out the harshest possible isolation, shut out life and love, everything that might have consoled him. But that wasn't punishment enough, she realized, horrified. Even if he didn't yet recognize it himself, he was bent on something darker, on the ultimate punishment, on some kind of self-destruction.

She had no idea how she knew such a thing. She even prayed that she was wrong, but the intuition was strong. Somewhere inside the man who enchanted children with his magic and repaired little girls' dolls there was a destructive force.

If it had been dormant in him before, it was alive now. It had opened a black pit of raging helplessness inside him. And unless something held back the darkness, it would consume him.

Unless *she* held back the darkness.

She walked to the bed and stood before him, her legs nearly giving way as she began to unbutton her blouse. She was offering herself to him, and they both knew it. It was the ultimate sacrifice for a woman with her store of self-pride and fanatical need for independence.

Her fingers felt icy and stiff as she tried to undo the first button. She was terrified that he might reject her. In his state of mine, Stephen Gage was quite capable of that final, crushing humiliation. But she had to take that chance.

"Shall I do this myself?" she said. "Or will you do it for me?" Emotion warred inside her—fear and anger, concern and compassion—all battling for control. Her eyes were drawn to him, to his desolation, to his nakedness as she freed the first button—and another impulse crept into her awareness. The stirrings of physical need. Desire. She hated herself for the inclination, but it was undeniable. She was as painfully drawn to him, as physically attracted now as the first day she'd met him.

His eyes clouded with pain as he watched her trembling attempt to save him. "For Heaven's sake, Lise . . . don't waste yourself this way."

"Waste myself?" Her voice was soft with surprise. "I've waited twenty-seven years for this moment, Stephen Gage. I think that's enough time wasted, don't you?"

For the first time in her life, Lise was glad that her breasts were full and generously made, that her body was rich with life, warm and soft. It would comfort him. It would bring him pleasure. She was glad for the gift of being a woman.

"I want to make love," she said, blushing delicately as her eyes drifted to his lower torso. "I want to do it *all*."

He exhaled as though in despair, but she saw the sparks leap in his smoldering blue eyes. She could almost see fire breathe from his nostrils.

"I'm not sure I can manage it *all*," he said savagely. "In my present condition."

"We'll work something out."

Despite her apparent nonchalance, the undressing was a slow and torturous affair for Lise. She had never undressed for a man. She had never done any of the things most women her age took for granted, and that damning knowledge made her awkward and clumsy.

"Come *here*," he said as she fumbled with the last few buttons on her blouse.

She sat beside him, a shiver rippling through her at the first touch of his hands. Though his fingers were tellingly rigid, he took his time finishing the unbuttoning ritual, and then he let her blouse hang open for a moment before he drew it off her shoulders. His eyes were slow and appreciative, blazingly blue as he lifted the front clasp of her bra. A grimace of a smile crossed his lips, and then with a flick of his thumb and forefinger, he released the catch.

His breath went ragged as the silky material sprang back and her breasts fell free.

Lise felt something give way deep inside her. Somewhere in the reaches of her belly, a trapdoor dropped open and dumped her bodily into sweet oblivion. She drew in a breath, frantic to regain some control, but it was the useless, reckless grasp of a falling woman. The air spun out of her lungs in a pleading sigh.

He opened his hand to cup her and breathed a single raw word. "I didn't know a woman could be this soft and beautiful."

"*I didn't know a woman could be this aroused,*" she whispered plaintively.

He met her eyes and claimed her breast with his long, burning fingers. "Do you know what you're doing, Miss Anderson?" His voice dropped to a harsh, thrilling whisper. "You're making me hot. I don't know if that's what you had in mind . . . but that *is* what you're doing."

Now Lise was *sure* she would never be able to breathe normally again. Sparks showered her insides as though he'd touched her with lightning. She felt melting heat, shocked excitement.

Even more astonishing were the shameless reactions of her virginal body. Her breasts strained for harder handling, and her private parts were clutchingly tight, shockingly damp. He was eating her alive with his eyes, but she wanted more than his hungry stare. She wanted his mouth and his hands and the hardened male pride that sprang from between his thighs.

"Making you . . . hot?" She could hardly breathe out the last word, and then she colored wildly under his hard stare. "Well . . . if that wasn't what I had in mind before . . . I think it probably is . . . now."

He didn't even give her time to take off her skirt.

"Leave it on," he said, pulling her to him. He began to draw the cotton material up as their mouths connected. The kiss was hard and sweet and full of his angry need. Lise was lost in it until he finally released her. She drew back, aware of the naked sensation of her breasts against his chest. *Brawn*, she thought again, feeling the hard crush of his muscles and the downy softness of his chest hair.

Her most acute awareness, however, was of her skirt bunched up around her hips, and his hand on her bare thigh.

"Come here," he said, swinging her around until she lay alongside him. He cupped her face, his fingers taut against soft flesh. Frustration was high in his eyes. Passion. Need. *Brutal need.*

"I'm trying like hell not to ravish you," he said, catching her under the arms and lifting her to him. "But if I'm winning the battle, I'm losing the war." With amazing strength, he held her above him as their lips touched and her breasts melted against his chest. The kiss was sweet and hot, but Lise ached for deeper contact. Her nipples pulled painfully as a low surge of need swept through her.

"I want to get lost in you, Lise," he said. "In your sweet mouth, in your lush body."

He settled her next to him and turned onto his side to face her, grimacing as he positioned himself. She felt like a crazy, wanton thing with her bra hanging open, her hair flying, and her skirt bunched around her waist. Her body *was* a wanton thing, clutching and throbbing with shameless desire.

"If you don't lose the damn battle soon," she said, her voice searingly husky, "I'm going to ravish *you.*"

"Is this Miss Anderson speaking?" A spark of laughter softened the harsh, sexual thrust of his voice, but only for an instant. The spark ignited in flames as he curved a hand to her hip and took her lips. He was abrupt and demanding, a man in a damn sexy rush. When he was finished with kissing her, he pulled her close, introducing her to the full, hard length of him.

Lise nearly expired with excitement. He was scorchingly hard as he rocked up against her, an overture to the slow, sensual thrusts of mating. The pressure was exquisite—heavy enough to arouse her, light enough to make her ache for more. She swallowed a gasp as he lifted her leg and hooked it over his hip. Was he going to make love to her this way?

Stephen had every intention of making love to her that way—on her side—but it wasn't the way he truly wanted to take her. In his dreams he wanted to roll onto his back and pull her astride him, rocking her until he was in so deeply that neither of them could move for fear of shattering. He wanted to forget where his body ended and hers began. He wanted her every way a man could have a woman.

And he wanted her now.

There was just one thing stopping him—both literally and figuratively. Her panties. They were the prim, white cotton panties of a virginal schoolteacher. And Miss Lise Anderson *was* a virginal schoolteacher. He was her first man! It didn't matter that she had a body lush enough for a burlesque queen. It didn't matter that he was half insane with needing her, he had to be patient. *He had to be gentle.*

The literal problem of her panties was easily solved.

As he eased the cotton crotch aside and stroked her with his fingers, she gasped and arched against him. He'd forgotten how tender and delicate a woman could be, how the petals turned to velvet under a man's touch. He aroused her the way a gentle breeze stirs an opening flower, with zephyrlike touches, whispering among her shell-pink folds and creases, swirling lightly over the hidden bud of sensation.

She tangled her hands in his hair and swore softly, anything but gentle. "Make love to me, Stephen," she said near his ear. "I'm ready, for heaven's sake. I most certainly *am.*"

Her desperation amused him almost as much as it aroused him. A schoolteacher to the last, he thought. Forever in charge. But she *was* ready. Her breasts felt flushed and taut against his arms, and the softness between her legs was dewy with moisture. Even the petals he caressed were exquisitely responsive, unfurling to receive him.

Lord knew *he* was ready. The aching hardness between his legs was a stick of dynamite with a lighted fuse, but he couldn't give into the tension just yet. He had to put off the pleasure a little longer. For both of them, but especially for her. "Ready isn't enough, Lise. You have to be on fire. You have to burn for it."

This was her first time, and he wanted her out of her mind with desire—so fever-hot and delirious, she wouldn't feel even the slightest physical twinge.

A low spasm gripped him as he thought about the explosive pleasure of taking her. *"Burn for it, Lise."*

He cupped her ample breast, aware of its weight and heat as he took the satin bud into his mouth. He drew on her tenderly, creating a cadence that pulled at something deep within him. It was the same primitive rhythm that beat in his body, and within seconds, he could feel the pain of desire mounting.

"I'm burning," she cried softly.

Every muscle in Stephen's body raged for release as he brought her legs up high around him and caught hold of her hips. "Grab hold of me, Lise," he said. "Hang on tight. I don't want to hurt you."

Lise grasped his shoulders as an unyielding force came up against the most vulnerable part of her body. So *this* was the mystery of sex, she thought. Her breath caught expectantly as he probed the throbbing softness between her legs. That same soft throb existed in every cell of her being. She could feel it building as he entered her, building with every sweet inch of space he took up within her. It riveted her senses, that beautiful throb. It enveloped her.

A kind of delirium overtook her as she began to breathe to the slow wonder of his magnificent invasion. He was good, she thought dazedly. *This* was good.

"Oh!!" The cry of pain was hers. She felt a quick, piercing sensation. For a second she could feel nothing else, and then the pressure eased, and she was filled with a stinging freedom that was oddly joyous.

"What are you doing to me?" she breathed. His mouth was hot on her breast and with each tug of his lips, she could feel a new urgency mounting. Within seconds she was moving against the hardness that had pierced her, urging it deeper. *The throb was in her, sweet and relentless.*

"I'm trying to do *this*," he said, holding her still as he eased into her slowly, gently, and very deeply. "There, now, how's that?"

"Ohh, Lord . . ." was all she could manage.

Pleasure rocked Lise's senses as he began to move. She felt it as a deep stirring within her body, a slow welling of sensation that made her realize she had never truly known the meaning of the word pleasure until now. It was more than pleasure, it was rapture. She didn't want the sweet pressure to stop. *Ever.* And then finally, when she was driven nearly crazy with the pure bliss of it, he gathered her to him and pressed into her body with thrilling force.

She cried out a sigh, clutching at him.

Stephen shuddered at the sound and abandoned all traces of gentleness, laying claim, *taking her.* His gut muscles fisted as she gave herself over totally to his vibrant strokes, wrapping her legs around him and pleading with him not to stop. He couldn't stop, not until he'd ravished her to within an inch of both their lives, not until they were spent and sighing . . . not until he'd taken her through the arc of blue light he could see in his mind.

He caught his breath, amazed as the light seemed to fan through his body, iridescent and pure. He imagined it streaming through both of them, expanding to envelop them. But what amazed him most was that he couldn't feel the pain of his injuries any longer. He couldn't feel anything but the racking shudders of their lovemaking.

"Hold me, Lise—"

He anchored her with his arms as he rolled to his back and pulled her astride him. Joy rocketed through him as she straddled him gracefully, taking him as deeply into her as it was possible for a man to penetrate a woman.

All reason fled him, all rational thought. She began to move above him, and everything that followed was a blinding glimpse of ecstasy. Her body was sheened with blue light. Her glowing loins brought him a pleasure so intense, it was metaphysical.

Somehow he knew when she was peaking. He'd lost track of everything else, of time and space, but her soft cry of pleasure galvanized him. One moment she was rocking above him, a crazy, beautiful goddess of the light, and the next she was folding in his arms, sobbing with joy.

He rolled her onto her back and drove into her one last time. The release that ripped through him was soundless and sublime, a comet soaring into eternity. There was no riot of bells or chimes. There were no exploding lights. Just the ecstasy he'd glimpsed. Blind ecstasy.

Her eyes were closed as he tilted her chin up moments later. He thought for a moment that she was sleeping, and then she let out a sigh and a smile. When she finally did open her eyes, they were dilated with pleasure. She looked as though she'd overdosed on mind-altering endorphins or drunk a bottle of straight happiness.

"Stephen, there are so many questions I want to ask you," she said.

He smoothed blond hair away from her face. "And I have a lot to tell you."

He'd no sooner got the words out than her eyes fluttered shut again, and she drifted off in his arms. He considered waking her—she was still half-dressed—but he couldn't bring himself to disturb her bliss. Let her sleep, he thought. There would be time enough later to deal with the rest of it.

He smoothed down her skirt and looped his arms around her, pulling her closer and wishing he could hold her that way forever. She felt like a part of him, as necessary to life as drawing breath. She was sunshine to a man who came from a world where the sun didn't exist. She was the only thing in *this* world he wanted.

A fiery pain pierced his heart as he glanced at her beautiful, peaceful expression. How the hell was he going to tell her, he wondered. And once he had, how was he going to live without her?

* * *

Lise had no idea what time of night it was when she awoke, but as she stretched and sighed softly, she became aware of two disturbing things . . . Stephen wasn't in bed with her, and the blue glow that filled the room had turned into a flaring beacon. It was so bright, she had to shield her eyes.

As her eyes adjusted she saw that it wasn't the rocks creating the strange aura. It was a beam of light that seeped from the storeroom. She straightened her clothing and found her blouse on the floor, hurrying to dress as a sense of uneasiness pervaded her.

The old door creaked in protest as she eased it open.

The room was dark except for the intense glow of digital readout displays and one pulsing shaft of brilliant light that shot straight up through an opening in the roof and into the night sky. Lise stared at it with rising alarm. It looked like some kind of space-age doomsday weapon, and for a moment she thought she was caught up in a waking nightmare.

She searched the room, agitation building. The incessant drone of feedback signals set her nerves on edge.

"Stephen! Where are you?"

An alarm signal shrilled and Lise's heart jolted violently.

From the far corner of the room, a figure rose out of the darkness. He stepped forward, blocking the brilliant light.

Lise began to back toward the door, suddenly terrified. "Stephen?"

Twelve

"Lise? You shouldn't be in here."

Lise was so relieved to hear Stephen's voice, she barely registered the urgency in his tone. "What's going on?" she said. "What are you doing?"

He moved toward her, a streaming shadow, and Lise felt a flash of genuine fear. "What's wrong?"

"The work I'm doing—" he said, pulling her with him out the door. "It's sensitive."

They ended up in the cabin's darkened living room. Stephen walked to the table by the window and switched on a student lamp. As the room warmed and shimmered with amber light, Lise felt the tightness in her chest ease slightly.

"I don't understand," she said. "You told me you were here because of the quarry lights."

"I am—but that's only part of it."

The window glass caught his reflection as he glanced out. It cast his features in an odd, opaque sheen, like light shining off water. Lise's breathing slowed. He didn't look like anything human at that moment.

"Stephen—" The question on her lips was so incredible, she didn't know how to ask it. "Are you a man? A normal man?"

"A man . . . ?" His surprise ended in a heavy expiration. "Sometimes I wonder. And as for normal? Who's to say?"

"But those marks on your body . . . the lightning. What do they mean?"

He turned to her in surprise, then glanced at the jeans he wore. "That's right. You took off my clothes, didn't you? That was only fair, I suppose. I seem to be removing yours often enough."

He settled himself on the table edge and waited until Lise took the room's only other chair, a creaky wooden rocker.

"So, you want to know about the thunderbolts," he said. "It's a bizarre story, Lise—in some ways, untellable. I'm not sure I even want to tell it. Or that you would believe it if I did."

Something had crept into the room's atmosphere. Lise could feel it prickle her skin, the uneasiness that came with not knowing what to expect. "Maybe I won't believe it," she said. "But at least give me a chance to decide that for myself. *Please.*"

He nodded at last. "All right, but first understand that I *am* a scientist. I don't believe in black magic or sorcery, but there are things in my past—incidents that I can't fully explain. Perhaps because of the nature of my work—or the location."

"Location?"

"Scandinavia—" He hesitated a moment, reflective. "The land of ice and fire. It was a few years after my wife died in childbirth. My field was extraterrestrial physics, and I'd been working under a NASA grant when an assignment came up to study the northern lights. My personal life was in shambles. I think if they'd offered me a job on the moon, I would have taken it, just to get away."

Lise was thunderstruck by the reference to Scandinavia. More than once she'd likened him to the gods of Nordic legend. But only in her thoughts, so he couldn't have known.

"I was based on the northern tip of Norway, and I'd only been there a few weeks when I had the bad judgment to tangle with a glacier. It was the dead of winter, and I got caught in a blizzard." His jaw tensed with self-deprecating laughter. "I fell into the crevasse of a glacier and landed head first on an ice sheet. I should have been dead—and when I came to, I thought I was."

"Why?" Lise prompted.

"I was in an ice cavern," he said. "Massive icicles hung everywhere, like crystal chandeliers. Outside of the aurora itself, it was the most incredible sight I'd ever seen. I don't remember anything else clearly except that there was an old Lapp with chamois for skin and snow-blown white hair chanting over me."

"A Laplander?" Lise recalled those stories from her childhood as well. Wonderful tales of fact and fancy about the small, sturdy people who occupied the north-lands of Norway, Sweden, and Finland.

"That was my guess, but he never introduced himself. He might have been a nomadic Lapp, or even a shaman. I was semiconscious most of the time, but I remember him holding the stones over me and chanting."

"The runes?"

"Yes. It seemed as if every time I opened my eyes he was dousing me in the blue phosphorescence the stones gave off. He kept chanting *Jumala* and *Ilmarinen*, and a third word that I recognized as lightning. I learned later that the first two words meant Lord of Sky, and that the old man was actually chanting Lord of Lightning. It was the name he'd given me."

"My goodness. What did you do to deserve such an exalted title?"

"I wish I knew," he said, laughing. "The study required me to be in Norway during the arctic winter— six months of perpetual darkness. Among other things, I shot pulse lasers into the aurora to study the effect. Maybe the old man saw the lasers and thought I was making lightning."

"Lord of Lightning," Lise said. "It's really rather beautiful. And he marked you with the lightning bolts?"

"I suppose it must have been him, although I don't remember it happening. I finally lapsed into total unconsciousness, and when I woke up, I was in a hospital in Narvik. I'd been found by another research team near the crevasse where I fell. I had a brain concussion, and when I tried to tell them what had happened, they didn't believe me. They thought I was hallucinating."

His quick shrug said that perhaps he agreed with them. "They also told me I should have been dead—and would have been if someone hadn't dragged me out of that glacier—and then found a way to relieve the cerebrospinal fluid building in my skull."

"The old man?" Lise couldn't hide her disbelief. "How did he do it?"

"There were no signs of surgery, primitive or otherwise. The stones are naturally magnetic—a legacy of the earth's volcanic origins. Their phosphorescence comes primarily from minerals that interact with the ultraviolet spectrum. In all honesty, I don't know," he said. "Maybe that combination has some stabilizing effect on the body's fluids."

"Is that possible?"

"Theoretically? No, probably not. But something happened. I found the stones in my parka pocket when I checked out of the hospital. The old man must have put them there." He rubbed his hand along his beard-shadowed jawline, an absent gesture. "I've stopped trying to make sense of it. I could almost convince myself it hadn't happened, except for the stones, the marks on my body—and the blinding headaches I still get."

His last reference triggered an insight. The headaches could account for those times when his eyes had lost focus and he'd seemed to be in a trancelike state, Lise realized. She needed a moment to digest all the information he'd given her.

"What sort of scientist studies the northern lights?" she asked finally.

"An auroral physicist, if you're curious about the exact title. The job takes me to some of the most inhospital spots on earth. My last tour of duty was Antarctica—the South Pole—three years of trial by ice."

He looked beyond her as though he was remembering. Lise could see the storm rising in his eyes, and it had all the bleakness of an arctic winter. She phrased a quick question in the hope of diverting his attention. "So that *is* why you're here? To study the quarry lights? You said they were like auroras."

He glanced out the window behind him, apparently checking the skies. "Your quarry lights are something of a mystery, Lise. Their electromagnetic properties are similar to auroras, and yet it's unusual to see the phenomena at altitudes this low. There are other possibilities, including the release of radon, combustible gases from the earth, or natural phosphorescence—"

He turned back and hesitated, as though deciding whether to go on. "The lights are only part of the reason I'm here. They're the symptom, not the cause. We're in the middle of an intense geomagnetic storm—"

"*We?*"

"The earth, Lise—the entire globe. This last week we were hit by a solar wind with a velocity up to two thousand kilometers per second. I'm talking about sunspots and solar flares—everything ol' Sol can throw at us. In other words, the sun is throwing a tantrum, and it's a beaut."

"Is it dangerous?"

"Not to human life at this point. But it's dangerous as hell to our worldwide electrical, navigation, and communications systems. That's the primary reason I'm here—to test a new laser communications device I designed. The Omega is built to withstand magnetic storms."

A laser, Lise thought. Not *Star Trek* or *Star Wars*. Not even *Starman*. He was testing a communications device, shooting lasers at . . . what? She pointed toward the roof of the cabin. "What's up there?" she asked.

"You've heard of the Space Shuttle? The Discovery crew is picking up my signals as we speak. Or at least I hope they are. This is the last night of their mission—and my last chance to test the Omega." He exhaled heavily. "So far the experiment has only been partially successful."

"But why would they send you *here* to test a laser?" Lise asked.

"Because of your quarry lights," Stephen explained. "They're emitting electromagnetic radiation in the range I needed for the tests.

A silence fell around them, bringing Lise alert. She experienced the fleeting surface chill that came with a premonition, and by the time she met his eyes, a trembling had started inside her.

"What is it, Stephen?" she asked.

He rose to his feet. "You understand that I have to leave."

Lise couldn't respond. The statement was too fraught with finality, with unthinkable implications.

"The Omega laser is my life's work," he explained. "If I can make it operational, the implications for ground- and space-based communication are"—he managed a grim smile—"at the risk of sounding dramatic, cosmic."

Her throat flared with pain. That certainly put it into perspective, didn't it? Cosmic wasn't a word a woman could argue with. She heaved a sigh. "When do you go?"

"Soon . . . I should leave tonight—as soon as the transmission is finished. There are modifications that have to be made to the system, and of course, more tests."

She searched his features for some indication of his feelings. Was he hurting too? Did the thought of leaving her tear him apart? The way it did her? What she saw in his eyes was an icy glimpse of infinity. The depth of his pain was limitless, beyond anything she could imagine.

"Where will you be going?" It was the only question she could think to ask.

He shook his head. "My work is highly sensitive, Lise. I've told you more than I should have already."

"But, you can't just disappear. Surely there's an address, a phone number . . . I mean—what if I wanted to contact you?"

"I can't be contacted."

His statement caught her like an elbow to the midsection. It knocked the wind out of her. She rebounded with a brittle burst of laughter and disbelief. "Oh, I see—then you'll write when you can—or call?"

He didn't answer, and Lise suddenly understood what the premonition had meant. He wasn't going to call. Ever.

The rocking chair gave a plaintive sound as she stood. *"I won't see you again, will I?"*

"Lise . . . my work is consuming. I'm on the brink of a breakthrough, perhaps one of the biggest in modern physics. There's nothing left over, no time."

The air she tried to draw into her lungs took on a sudden, crushing weight. His work, she thought, his *life's* work. That was reason enough for any man to sidestep a relationship, she supposed. If that was the real reason.

She nearly flinched with pain as she looked at him. He'd risen to his full height, and his eyes had crystallized to ice, inured to the hurting. Though it was the last thing Lise wanted at that moment, she found it impossible not to respond to him. His physical size, his presence, everything about him signified boundless strength. And yet the fatal flaw she'd once predicted was there, carved into his gaunt bones. He was a man divided. A man locked in mortal conflict—with himself.

"Stephen, if you have to leave, I won't try to stop you. But *please*, tell me the real reason."

Anger flashed through him, galvanizing him. "Your father destroyed your mother's life—that's what you said, wasn't it? That he was a domineering bastard? Well, I'm a domineering bastard too. A woman died because she couldn't say no to me. I pressured her into a relationship, into marriage, even pregnancy before she was ready. She's *dead*, Lise." He turned away on a harsh sound. "The baby's dead."

"Stephen, don't you think it's time—"

He whirled on her, furious. "To forgive myself? For Lord's sake, don't feed me platitudes! It isn't about forgiving myself. It's about knowing who I am. It's about living with the knowledge that I can destroy people with my own selfish urges—that I have that power."

"You don't destroy people—you *help* them. Look what you did for my students, and for Em."

He shook his head wearily. "Your students took me for an alien—or have you forgotten? The whole town did. Maybe they saw something you wouldn't let yourself see." He indicated his beard and shaggy lion-gold hair. "Take a look at me, Lise. I *am* an alien. I don't belong here in this world—in *your* world. I've been away too long, from people, from life."

A wave of longing rocked her as she met his angry gaze. "I know what I see." She saw a man torn by guilt, but he was still the most wonderful man she'd ever known, the *only* man she'd ever wanted to give herself to. If he was angry and alienated, he was also capable of warmth and great tenderness. Even now he was beautiful to her eyes—rugged and strong and golden. He was the hero of her childhood daydreams.

Her heart quickened with the need to persuade him that he was wrong, but she couldn't bring herself to speak. The future was clearly defined in his unyielding expression. He was going to leave her. He *had* to leave.

"Lise, I can't do it," he said, his voice hard and aching. "Don't ask me to try. It will kill us both. I can't live here with you, and I can't take you with me."

She nodded, her heart twisting. He was pleading with her to understand. Even if he could make peace with himself, even if his work wasn't an issue, he didn't believe himself capable of making the adjustment to her life—to small-town life—perhaps even to happiness. He had chosen self-exile. It was his path, his penance.

She became aware of the rocker creaking behind her. It was still teeter-tottering from her sudden departure, and the anguished sound brought an ache to her throat. What did she do now? Leave? That would be the civilized way to handle it. Make her good-byes, *somehow*. Leave before her emotions betrayed her.

"I think I left my shoes"—she jerked a hand toward the bedroom—"in there."

Stephen watched her go with a suffocating sense of loss. The dull pain that throbbed at the base of his skull built to splitting proportions, and his hands fisted. He had to restrain himself from putting one of them through the wall.

She was fumbling into her sandals when he entered the room. He told himself not to speak to her, or touch her. He had no right. He had to let her go.

A low moan of despair came out of her as she flung the offending sandal aside and then hobbled over to retrieve it.

"Let me get it," he offered.

She pivoted, startled. "No!" She knelt to get the shoe and stayed down on the floor, tucked into a crouch. "Go away, Stephen, please. Don't make this any harder."

"Harder?" He let out a sound riddled with frustration. "Ah, Lise, this is tearing my *heart* out. It couldn't *be* any harder. I don't want to leave you," he said raggedly.

She glanced up at him, disbelieving. "You don't?"

"*No,* I don't. I feel as though I'm losing part of myself, something irreplaceable, but—"

"I know, I know," she said, a throaty break in her voice, "you have to go." She rose, her dawn-blue eyes swimming with tears.

They stood apart, staring at each other helplessly, until finally Stephen spoke. "What do we do now?"

"We say good-bye."

"Yes . . . but how?"

A sad smile touched her lips, and then it wavered and broke into something soft and heartbreakingly radiant. "You could make love to me . . . one last time."

The shock that flared through him was a physical force. But it was her expression that struck at his soul. She was so open, so achingly vulnerable, he couldn't move for a moment. Every emotion played on her face exquisitely—love, pain, longing. She was risking it all. Lise Anderson was a woman defenseless, naked. There was nowhere for her to hide.

He took the shoe from her hand, tossed it aside, and dragged her into his arms. As they clung to each other their eyes squeezed shut, and he let out the butchered sound that was locked inside him. His heart felt strangled as he pulled back and kissed her tear-streaked lashes. She had unlocked all the torment inside him. She had laid open the wounds.

Lovemaking was out of the question. They both knew it would be too painful to bear. And yet they couldn't part without knowing the raging sweetness again. He touched her face, a question in his eyes, and at her silent nod, he picked her up and carried her to the bed.

They were lovers stunned and slowed by the immediacy of their responses. Each point of contact was so exquisitely charged that they barely had to touch. When they did come together, it was with a shellburst of longing. Their coupling was graceful and poignant. It was searingly silent. They were made mute by feelings, neither of them able to say the words of love their bodies expressed so eloquently.

It was the most beautiful, painful interlude of Stephen's life, and he knew by its end that he would have her with him always. She was indelible, as much an element of life as the breaking dawn. When his world was ice and darkness, she would be there, like the dawn, lighting his way.

He was gone when Lise awoke the next morning. The first thing she did when she touched her feet to the floor was walk to the storeroom and open the door. The room was empty, and her immediate response was denial. How could he possibly have moved his equipment without waking her? A dozen other questions stormed her mind until she released them all with a sigh of resignation. Stephen Gage wasn't subject to a normal man's flaws, or his limitations. Even though he denied it, he had some kind of magic on his side.

He *was* gone, however, every trace of him. That couldn't be denied. Sadness welled up inside her. One lonely tear shimmered, full of heartache as it caught on her lower lash. She felt as empty and abandoned as the room.

Moments later she stood at the window, staring out at the pristine morning. Sunlight filtered through the treetops, promising a warm and lazy summer day. There was no sign of yesterday's violence, no sign of a raging magnetic storm. Life in Shady Tree went on, she thought. He had come and gone, leaving the place untouched. Only she had changed.

A sparrow hawk was perched on the porch railing, its head cocked oddly as it stared at her. There was something so personal about the bird's scrutiny, Lise was reminded of Em's claim that the spaceman had brought a dead bird to life. She'd dismissed it then as a figment of the child's imagination. Now she didn't know. Now anything seemed possible. Perhaps she and the curious little sparrow hawk had something in common. Perhaps they'd both been touched by lightning.

She was dressing to leave when she noticed what looked like a paper ID tag on the floor near the storeroom door. Thinking it might have been torn off Stephen's equipment, she picked it up and read the scrawled numbers. They weren't in any sequence or combination she recognized, but on the chance that it was something he'd lost or forgotten, she tucked the tag in her purse.

A short time later, as she drove off in her car, she glanced at her watch and saw that it had stopped. The hands were frozen at midnight. Sadness gripped her again, squeezing her heart. She had forgotten to ask him how he did that—stopped watches. *Stopped time.* Now she would never have the chance.

Thirteen

"Thirty-six bottles of root beer on the wall! Thirty-six bottles of root beer—"

The windows of the old school bus rattled with the deafening enthusiasm of Abraham Lincoln's fifth-grade class. The students were headed for the L.A. Sports Arena that bright summer morning to compete in the Southern California Junior Science Fair. Julie was stationed at the front of the bus, leading the boisterous bunch in song, while Lise sat at the back, keeping a watchful eye on things.

She winked as Em Baxter glanced over at her from across the aisle. The little girl's odd behavior recently had forced Lise to set aside her own heartaches. Em had been quiet and listless all week, withdrawing into herself. Lise suspected it had something to do with Stephen's leaving, but when she'd tried to talk to the child, Em had simply stonewalled. "He'll come back," she'd said. "And when he does, I'm going to ask him to show me how to make birds fly."

Lise's smile saddened. Em had such unwavering faith in the "spaceman" that Lise could hardly bear the thought of seeing her disappointed. She still hadn't found a way to tell Em he wasn't coming back. At the time she'd simply drawn the child into her arms and hugged her.

"Twenty-five bottles of root beer on the wall—"

Her students' high spirits reclaimed Lise's attention, and by the time the noisy contingent had arrived at the Sports Arena, everyone's attention was riveted on setting up their "Train of the Future." Perhaps because there was so much at stake, the spirit of teamwork prevailed. A common cause does wonders, Lise thought, as she bent over the three-part informational display that would sit behind the railroad pike.

She felt a tug on the back pocket of her jeans as she mounted a "before" picture of the maglev. "What is it, Em?" she said, not bothering to look behind her. She knew Em's preferred modus operandi by now.

"Do you think we'll win, Miss Anderson?"

"Yes," Lise said almost immediately. "I'm sure we will." She set down the glue and turned to the little girl. Em's gray eyes were wide with surprise, and Lise realized she'd surprised even herself. Normally she wouldn't have risked raising the child's hopes for fear of disappointment, but perhaps it was Em's own faith that had prompted her. Every so often a strong dose of hope was necessary, she realized. Maybe believing was the only antidote to grim reality.

She drew Em over to see the display. "This is why I think we should win," she said, detailing the features that made their maglev project unique among model trains. "And what's more," she added moments later, winding up her spiel, "in the real world, a maglev train would require less energy, produce no smog *and* relieve traffic congestion on the freeways."

Em blinked. "I guess we can't lose, huh?"

Lise nodded and sent the little girl off to help one of the volunteer mothers who was distributing midmorning juice and snacks. *Please don't let me be wrong,* she thought.

The rest of the morning proceeded in the same spirit of impending triumph. Once Lise's class had the maglev project set up and operational, she took her students on a tour of the other displays. There were several projects on computers, one on optical illusions, and one called "Motion of the Ocean" that was so bril-

liantly conceived Lise began to worry she'd overesti-
mated their chances.

Lunch was a festive affair with an all-you-can-eat
pizza buffet, ice-cream cake for dessert, and an ex-
NASA astronaut who spoke to the children about the
future of space exploration. His talk made Lise think
of Stephen, and she was trying to shake off her melan-
choly mood when Julie rushed up.

"Lise, it's Em!"

Julie was so shaken that Lise sprang to her feet to
steady the girl. "What about Em?" she demanded, pulling Julie out of earshot of the children's table.

"She felt sick and asked me to take her to the rest
room." Julie let out a moan of near anguish. "She vom-
ited, Lise—blood, I think. She's in terrible pain!"

By the time Lise burst into the rest room, she had
reached a state of nerves that transcended hysteria.
Under other circumstances she might have fallen apart
at the sight of Em Baxter's body crumpled on the rest-
room floor, but some higher signal in her brain told
her to kneel, to take the child's pulse.

"Julie, call an ambulance—*quickly*," Lise said, pressing her fingers to the carotid artery in Em's neck. The
child's pulse was faint and thready. She was unconscious, Lise realized. And burning up with fever. Food
poisoning? Blood poisoning? Other possibilities
assaulted Lise, even more horrific.

She wouldn't allow herself to think the thought that
flashed into her head. Em would be all right. The child
had a spirit as abiding as the Olympic flame. The light
in her solemn gray eyes was inextinguishable. Lise had
Em's destiny all mapped out, she realized. She was
going to live to be one hundred and two—and maybe
even teach school at Abraham Lincoln. She *would* be
all right.

Lise was oblivious to the siren's shrieks as she sat
next to Em in the ambulance. She held the child's
hand tightly, trying to transfuse her with lifeblood, or

vital energy, or whatever intangible thing it was that kept people alive.

The paramedics hadn't been able to diagnose the child's condition except to say that it was critical, so Lise was fighting an invisible enemy. Whatever malaise had gained a foothold in Em's frail body, it was powerful and insidious. Her pulse was wildly erratic now—racing one moment, barely detectable the next. Despite the ice the paramedics had packed her in, her temperature was soaring.

"Come on, Em, *fight*," Lise whispered.

Lise had always found it difficult to believe in the intangibles others took for granted, but she did believe in the sanctity of life. Em Baxter was not going to die. *Not today. Not this way.* The child represented something Lise couldn't put into words. What had Stephen said about her? She was a mirror to life's hope, to its—Lise had forgotten the rest of his remark, but it didn't matter. He'd obviously meant that Em was special in someway. That she was protected.

Lise squeezed the child's hand and thought she felt an answering pressure. The eerie calmness that had enveloped Lise fled. Her heart started beating wildly. "Em? Emily?" she said, squeezing again. Had the child actually responded? Lise's own thundering excitement was hampering her ability to discern the subtle feedback she was looking for. She had to calm down!

"Emily?" Leaning closer, Lise saw a twitch of movement in the child's mouth. Her lips parted slightly as though she were trying to say something.

"Dah . . ."

"What is it, Em?" Lise searched her memory for a connection as the child murmured the sound again. "What, Em? Your *doll*? Is that what you want? I have it right here."

Grateful she'd remembered to bring the doll with her, Lise tucked it into the curve of the five-year-old's arm. "There you go, sweetheart."

The child stirred slightly, her eyelids quivering.

"It's okay, Em," Lise said as the child's eyes drooped

open for a moment. "You're going to be okay. Can you hear me? It's Miss Anderson. I'm with you—"

A nerve twitched in Em's cheek. She was struggling to stay conscious. "Is he . . . here?" she asked.

"He?" Lise gripped the child's hand tighter, realizing who she meant. "No, sweetheart, Stephen had to go away. He was called away, honey. Em?"

Em's eyes had drifted shut again. "He'll come back," she whispered. "He'll fix me . . . like he fixed Elizabeth."

Lise swallowed against something hot and acrid in her throat.

A moment later the ambulance came to a halt, the back doors swung open to a blinding explosion of neon light, and paramedics swarmed inside. Emily's hand was torn from hers, and Lise was pushed forcefully aside as the team lifted the little girl's body to a gurney.

"Wait! Will she be all right?" Lise cried as they rolled the gurney out of the van. "*Please!* Let me go with her!"

Someone thrust Em's doll into Lise's hands. "Take it easy, ma'am," one of the paramedics said. "Are you her mother?"

"No—her teacher."

He directed Lise through the same doors they'd just wheeled the gurney. "Right through there, ma'am. They'll want some information from you."

Lise had finished with the admittance people and was in the hospital's waiting area when Julie arrived with Danny Baxter.

"Where's Em?" Danny said, going pale with fear as he took in Lise's appearance. "Where is she, Miss Anderson? Is she all right?"

Lise swept back damp hair from her forehead aware that she must look frightening. "She'll be fine, Danny, just fine. They're taking care of her right now. They'll let us know as soon as they have something to report."

Lise settled Danny in a chair and caught Julie's eye, indicating with a nod of her head that she wanted to talk to her alone. Once they were in the hallway, Lise began a series of hushed, rapid-fire instructions.

"Call Em and Danny's mother, Julie, and tell her what's happened. Be careful not to frighten her—and let her know that I'm here with Em. Then you go back to the fair and round up the kids. You and the volunteer mothers will have to be in charge of getting them home safely. And take Danny with you. He's frightened out of his mind, and he's much too young to be stranded here in this hospital."

She patted Julie's arm and forced what she hoped was a reassuring smile. "Are you okay, sport? Can you handle all that?"

"Hey—I'm fine, teach—but *you've* looked better." Julie drilled her with a stare. "How is Em, really? And none of that 'she's fine' stuff. Tell me the truth."

Lise fought to keep her voice steady. "Her condition is critical. They don't know what's wrong yet."

"Ms. Anderson?"

Both Lise and Julie turned as a young doctor rushed up. "Ms. Anderson, the little girl we just admitted to Emergency has a suppurating appendix. She's going to require immediate surgery. They're prepping her now. Are you a relative?"

"No, but I've given your admittance people her mother's name. They're trying to contact her now."

The doctor wiped a trickle of sweat from his brow. "I'm going to need some background," he said. "Do you know anything about the child's medical history? Has she ever exhibited symptoms of nausea, vomiting, or abdominal pain before?"

Lise was about to say no when she remembered the day she'd gone to the Baxter house and found Em sick in bed with flu symptoms. Even the doctor she'd called had assured her Em would be fine with some bed rest. Everything *had* indicated the flu, Lise told herself. She had handled it responsibly. And yet the guilt that flashed through her was nearly immobilizing. If she'd taken Em in for a checkup that day or told her mother she needed one, if she'd paid closer attention to her since, maybe none of this would have happened!

Julie stepped forward. "Is Em going to be all right?" she asked.

The doctor addressed himself to Lise. "The child's condition is critical, Ms. Anderson. There are symptoms of peritonitis. We're doing everything we can."

"Peritonitis?" The word splintered the shell of clam Lise had built around herself. *We're doing everything we can.* She knew what that meant. It meant there was damn little they *could* do.

Somehow she managed to answer the rest of the doctor's questions, and then she sank to a chair. Julie crouched next to her as the doctor left.

"Lise—now don't *you* fall apart!" Julie said fiercely. "Em's going to need you."

"I'm all right." She waved Julie away. "You go, take Danny."

"No way. I'm staying until you snap out of this. If you're blaming yourself, Lise, I want you to stop it right now. Stop this craziness, Lise! Do you hear me?"

Lise shook her head. Julie's words were as garbled and meaningless as a foreign language. She couldn't collect her thoughts. She couldn't stop shaking inside. Seconds flew by before she could meet her teaching assistant's troubled gaze. "She asked for him, Julie. She believes he can fix her the way he did her doll."

"What do you mean? Em asked for someone? Who?"

"Stephen. The spaceman."

"The spaceman?" Julie sprang to her feet. "For heaven's sake, Lise—*call* him! Get him over here!"

Lise shook her head helplessly. "I don't know where to reach him."

Julie scanned the hall and pointed to a phone booth. "Come on!" she cried. "We've got to reach him! It doesn't matter whether he can really fix Em or not. She *believes* he can."

Julie thumbed through the phone book while Lise paced and searched her memory for any clue Stephen might have given as to where he was going. She recalled him mentioning NASA, and then she remembered something else—the equipment tag.

She found the tag in her purse, tucked in the zipper

compartment where she'd placed it for safekeeping. The scrawled numbers still looked foreign to her, but as she held the paper out for Julie to see, she realized what it was.

They both spoke at once. "It's a phone number."

The dash was omitted after the prefix, Lise realized, making it look more like a serial number or some other form of ID.

"I'll call him," she told Julie. "Don't worry, I'll find him, I *will*. You go now. Take care of the kids, okay?"

Once Julie and Danny had left, Lise tried the number. She wasn't even sure she had the right area code, and when the phone began to ring, it startled her. Her stomach went nervously light as she realized she might actually be talking to Stephen at any moment. The days that had passed since she'd seen him felt like months. In some ways he seemed a stranger. And yet she felt sure that once she'd impressed upon him how serious Em's condition was, he would come immediately. *He had to.*

The phone rang several times before a woman picked it up and repeated the seven digits Lise had just dialed. "How can I help you?" she asked.

"I was told I could reach Stephen Gage at this number."

"Stephen Gage? Who's calling?"

"My name is Lise Anderson. It's important."

"Just a moment—"

Lise was aware of a soft, continual clicking as she waited for the woman to come back on the line. She was also aware of the receiver, slick and cold against her hand.

"I'm sorry," the woman broke in abruptly. "This is the switchboard. The facility *is* closed, and I'm not authorized to give out any more information over the phone."

"Can you tell me if he works there? It's an emergency—"

"I have no listing for that name, ma'am. I'm not authorized to say more. Thank you for calling."

A dial tone discouraged Lise from further questions.

No listing. She sighed heavily and considered her options, which had just dwindled from one to none. It was too big a haystack, she realized, despairing. He could be anywhere, including the Arctic circle.

She glanced down the hall, saw the double doors of the operating room, and froze. Em was in there now, she realized, her fate in the hands of strangers—nameless, faceless people who didn't know how important their five-year-old patient was. They couldn't know. They'd never been privileged to see her regarding the world with her serious, gray eyes. They'd never been the recipients of her wistful smile . . . on those occasions when she did smile. They didn't know she was a tiny, steady light against the darkness.

Oh, please. A wave of helplessness crashed over Lise. *Please,* she thought, her mind reaching into the operating room. *Save her. I want to see that smile again.*

Moments later Lise sat tucked in a molded plastic chair in the waiting area, afraid to move. She wanted to shudder, but she forced the impulse away. It might unlock the trembling shakiness inside her. Her nose stung like fire and her jaw ached, but it was better than the alternative. She was too full of anguish. Losing control now would destroy her.

Lise had no idea how much time had passed when she heard someone coming down the hall with a quick, deliberate cadence. She expected the footsteps to pass the waiting room, another doctor or nurse on the run. But they didn't. They hesitated and entered the room, approaching her as she sat huddled in meditation.

"Lise?"

Lise looked up, her heart beating oddly.

Julie hovered over her, pale and frightened. "Lise? What's wrong? Is it Em? Has something hap—"

"No," Lise said quickly. "There's been no word since they took her into surgery."

"What about Stephen?"

"I couldn't reach him." Lise's chin began to tremble and she looked away, making a pretense of checking her watch. As she noticed the time she realized she'd been at the hospital for two hours. "What are you doing here, Julie?" she said. "You're supposed to be on your way home with the kids."

"We won, Lise."

"What?" Confused by Julie's excitement, Lise rose to her feet. "What are you talking about?"

"Our maglev took top honors at the science fair. We won the scholarship, Lise. We won!"

"Oh, Julie." Lise had such mixed emotions. She was thrilled, and at the same time, deeply saddened. She wanted to share the triumph with all her students. They'd exceeded her dreams—and probably their own. But there could be no triumph without Em.

Julie's smile faded, as though she'd read Lise's mind. "Em would be very happy about this," she managed awkwardly.

"*Will* be happy," Lise corrected.

The two women stood a moment, unable to find the right words. Finally Lise pulled Julie into her arms, and they hugged fiercely. Lise thought her heart would break as the tears she'd been fighting welled up.

"She *will* be happy," Julie whispered.

Stephen clenched his fist, locking off the satisfaction of putting it through the nearest wall. The familiar array of his equipment sprawled before him, only now the bank of monitors was dark and the perpetual electronic whirring had been silenced. He'd just pulled the plug on the entire system. What had kept him from destroying it, he didn't know.

There was a flaw in his design somewhere, a fatal error that eluded him. It was the kind of problem that would have totally absorbed him a year ago. Now, staring at the maze of cold steel and circuits, all he wanted was to take a sledgehammer to it. *To hell with the whole noble endeavor,* he thought savagely.

He breathed in deeply, feeling the pain that had been with him since she'd left her, the searing ache in his heart, the rip of claws through his gut. She was there in his mind, just as he'd known she would be . . . eyes as pale blue as dawn, hair the color of ripe wheat. He could see the freckles on her nose, the proud tilt of her head.

He could almost reach out and touch her.

Lord, he could almost give it all up for her! *Almost.* That was what was killing him. Much as he might want to vent his rage, much as he might want to destroy the Omega, or walk away from it, he couldn't— not and still live with himself. He'd come too close. It would haunt him.

His head began to throb, and again he resisted the violent pleasure of putting his fist through the wall. Instead he hit the light switch, plunging the room into darkness. He'd had these black rages before. He had lived with episodes of terrible despair. They went away in time. *This one would too.*

In the background of his thoughts a telephone began to ring, its shrill, harsh and insistent. It would be the facility with a message, but he had no interest in talking to one of their anonymous female operators at the moment.

He let it ring.

Fourteen

"Ms. Anderson?"

Lise turned as the doctor entered the waiting area. "Emily's in intensive care," he said. "The appendix we removed was badly abscessed. We're treating her with intervenous antibiotics, but we haven't been able to bring her fever down."

"Will she be all right?" Lise asked.

He looked suddenly haggard. "We're doing all we can."

Lise turned away as he left, her heart pounding. She tried to force away the dread that swamped her, but the feeling was too strong. As she sank to the chair a horrible realization took hold. Em was dying.

She had no sense of time passing as she sat there, slumped against the wall, though hours might have slipped by. She was trapped in the agony of waiting, stunned by it. The sun had begun to fall, and the small room, which had been quiet all day, was now completely deserted.

Perhaps it was the chill passing over her skin that roused her. She heard no unfamiliar sounds, nothing out of the ordinary . . . and yet she felt the presence of someone else in the room. She looked up, scanning empty air. She was alone, but her heart began to pound. Had someone said her name? She could hear it resonating softly in her mind.

"Stephen?"

She had the sudden and intense feeling that he was near. A moment later she was rushing into the hallway, impelled by the impulse. "Where's the recovery room?" she called out as an orderly appeared. He pointed her down the hallway past the operating room. She reached double doors that said No Admittance and pushed through them. Only one bed was occupied—a small child in an oxygen tent. It was Em. Standing over her was a golden-haired man in a red flannel shirt.

Lise whispered the name. *"Stephen?"*

"Ma'am? You can't come in here!" A nurse moved to block Lise's path, and then the orderly appeared. Lise was propelled gently but firmly through the doors she'd entered.

"No! Please—I have to talk to him," she pleaded as the doors closed behind her.

The orderly looked confused. "Who, ma'am? The doctor? He's not in there."

"No, Stephen—" She glanced through the door's window, pointing toward the child's bed. What she saw froze her in disbelief and confusion. It *was* Em in the oxygen tank, but no one stood next to her. Stephen wasn't there. Lise felt another chill burn her skin. Maybe he'd never been there. Maybe she'd imagined him.

She caught hold of her arms, trying to make sense of what had happened when she heard someone say her name, a resonant male voice that came from behind her.

"Lise?"

She swung around, a gasp in her throat.

He stood at the juncture of two hallways, his golden hair aflame, his red flannel shirt a beacon in the drab surroundings. Lise pressed her hand to the wall, steadying herself as he walked toward her. "Do you see him too?" she asked the orderly, terrified that she was imagining things again.

"Yes, ma'am, I do." The orderly's whisper spoke of

awe, as though he knew he was in the presence of something magical.

Suddenly Stephen was there, his hand gripping hers, warm and life-giving, his strength flowing through her.

"Lise, I came as soon as I could—"

Lise's eyes welled with tears as she searched the concern etched in his rugged features. She didn't bother to ask him how he knew where to find her. "Em needs you, Stephen. *Hurry.*"

Stephen could feel the life force ebbing out of the unconscious child as he stood over her. An oxygen mask covered her mouth and nose; monitors measured her faltering vital signs. Outside, Lise waited with Em's mother and Danny, who had just arrived with Julie. There were so many people whose lives this child had touched, Stephen thought. And so many more lives she could still touch if she lived.

He caught hold of her hand, enfolding it in his as he tried to project his thoughts into her mind. "Come back, Em," he said. "Come back to us. It's not your time to return to stardust."

The sparkling light that enveloped Em was warm and beautiful. It seeped into her being, filling her with peace and contentment. It bathed her in a love beyond anything she'd ever known. She watched with delight as the light gently spun away from her and shot upward, arcing across an indigo sky. Vibrant colors danced in its path, every color the eye could see and some it couldn't even imagine. The light was a rainbow, Em realized, and she was meant to follow it to the treasure.

A man called her name as she began her journey. His voice was familiar, and she smiled as a form materialized out of the darkness.

"Are you coming with me, Spaceman?" she asked him.

"No, Em, it's not my time. I can't go with you."

"Would you like to, though?"

"Someday, Em. Yes, someday, I would like to go. Right now, there's someone I don't want to leave behind."

"You mean Miss Anderson?"

He nodded. *"Are you sure you want to leave her behind, Em? Or Danny and your mom?"*

Em thought that over a long time. *"I'd like to leave Danny behind,"* she said. *"Sometimes he teases me."*

The spaceman smiled then, and Em was glad. He'd looked so sad before. For the first time, Em noticed he was carrying her doll. *"Can Elizabeth come with me?"* she asked.

"Sure . . . I'd think she'd like that."

He handed her the doll, and as Em tucked it under her arm, she felt a tug of sadness. She didn't want to leave her mother behind, not really. She didn't want to leave Miss Anderson either. She would miss them all, even Danny. She contemplated the spaceman's deep blue eyes. *"If I don't follow the rainbow this time,"* she said. *"I mean if I came back to Shady Tree instead, would you show me how to make birds fly?"*

Lise and Stephen stood apart from each other in the waiting area. Even Danny and Mrs. Baxter were separated by several chairs, and Julie had taken up a post near the snack machine. Five excruciating hours had passed since Stephen had returned from Em's bedside, and still there'd been no change in her condition.

Lise was numbed by despair. She'd been so sure that Stephen's presence would bring about a miracle. Perhaps they all had been. Now it seemed they'd reached the stage where they weren't even able to console each other.

"Mrs. Baxter?" The young doctor's voice was faint as he entered the room. He looked as though he'd aged ten years in a single day.

Em's mother turned to him, fear in her eyes. Lise felt it, too, gut-wrenching fear. They all did.

A heavy sigh drained out of him as he nodded at Mrs. Baxter. "Your daughter's taken a turn for the better, ma'am. Her vital signs have stabilized."

The woman rose to her feet unsteadily. "Emily's going to be all right?"

The doctor nodded. "Yes, we think so."

Lise's eyes filled with tears, and she pressed a trembling fist to her mouth, unable to control the gratefulness that rocked through her. The vigil was over. Her legs swayed beneath her as she turned to Stephen and held out a hand.

He was there as she turned, moving toward her in a red-and-gold blur of motion, his eyes full of relief and crazy passion. He was there, catching her in his arms, breaking her tilting, teetering fall. He was there, whispering the most incredible things in her ear, telling her how thankful he was that Em was okay, telling her how much he loved her.

All the emotion Lise had held back broke free in one aching wave. If Stephen hadn't been holding her, she would have sagged to the floor. There was no way to salvage her schoolteacher's dignity, no way to stop the tears. She cried for the joy she felt, for the pain they'd all been through. She wept for Em's rebirth, and for the child's future. And somehow in the sweet, sobbing aftermath of it all, she remembered those three words Stephen had whispered.

What had he said? In all the upheaval, it seemed entirely possible to her that she was hearing things again. Somehow she mustered the strength to draw back and search his face. "Stephen? . . . What did you say?"

He blotted her tears with his fingers and gazed at her, his features blazingly tender. "I said Em is okay—"

"No, I mean that other thing."

He scooped her up, turning with her in his arms and nearly squeezing the breath out of her with his stormy passion. As he set her back down, he pressed his lips to her temple and breathed out a husky groan of masculine need. "I love you, Lise."

She had definitely heard that. And so had everyone else in the room. Julie and Danny and Mrs. Baxter were staring at her and Stephen with bewildered expressions.

It took Lise a moment to clear the ringing dizziness from her head. *Em was safe . . . Stephen was holding her, telling her he loved her?* Was any of that possible? As soon as she could manage it, she disentangled from Stephen's arms to address her astonished audience.

"Could you excuse us a moment?" she asked, her legs barely navigating as she drew Stephen with her toward the door. "Please, I know this isn't exactly appropriate, but I—*we*—need some—time. Alone."

"Well, okay," Julie said, grinning. "I guess maybe Flash Gordon can be trusted. I got a postcard from the Davenport sisters this morning. It was postmarked Acapulco, not Mars."

Danny Baxter looked quite sincere in his concern. "Maybe you shouldn't, Miss Anderson. I know they caught Buck Thompson with those museum statues in his trunk and everything, but the other morning I noticed some funny-looking pods in the backyard, and—"

"Go," Mrs. Baxter ordered, pulling her son close and shushing him with a hug. "Talk it out, you two. Or whatever it is you have to do."

As soon as they'd escaped the oppressive confines of the hospital for the cool evening air outside, Stephen pulled Lise back into his arms. "What am I going to do with you, Lise? What am I going to do *about* you?"

Lise pressed her hand to his shirt and felt the heavy thud of his heart. An aching tightness rose in her chest. She had never loved anyone so much that it hurt even to breathe.

"That's easy"—she cleared her throat, but the hoarseness wouldn't go away—"You could marry me, live here, and teach science at Abraham Lincoln. We need a good science teacher."

Pain flashed through his golden features. "I *can't*, Lise. You know I can't."

Lise closed her eyes, tears welling. Her heart was going to break, dammit. It was going to crack right in two. She wouldn't live through it if he left her again, especially now, after telling her he loved her. "Well, then," she said, barely managing a grainy whisper, "you could always commute."

"From the Arctic circle?"

She opened her eyes and looked up at him, all the misery inside her rushing into her words. "Yes, why *not* from the Arctic circle. Why not from the moon if you have to? Do you want to be with me or don't you, Stephen?"

He gripped her tighter, searching her features. "Lise, are you serious? I could only get back a few times a year—"

"That's better than the alternative."

"Do you know what you're saying? That you'll wait for me?" His eyes blazed with fire, with hope. "I can't ask you to do that, Lise. I don't know how long it's going to take me to get the laser operational—"

"One thing at a time. Can you stay tonight?"

"Yes—yes, I'll stay the weekend. Hell, I'll postpone my next test and stay the week!"

She laughed as he pulled her close and hugged the breath out of her. She laughed and cried and wondered if she could survive a bipolar relationship with a stormy Viking god of a man. "No need to be rash," she whispered.

He held her in his arms, caressing her hair and thrilling her with husky, heartfelt promises. He told her he didn't exist without her, that she would be his sunlight when he was away. He told her he *would* come back someday, to live in Shady Tree, to marry her, maybe even teach science.

Wait for him? she thought, sighing rapturously. How silly could he be? She would have put herself in a deep freeze if necessary. She would wait until Johnny Carson was canceled or the sun burnt out, whichever came first.

Lise might have been totally content in his arms, her face soaked with tears, her thoughts floating in bliss, if only it weren't for the unanswered questions creeping back into her awareness.

"How did you find me, Stephen?" she murmured against his red flannel shoulder. "And how did you know Em was sick?"

He stroked her hair. "Sorry, Miss Anderson, but a man in my line of work has to keep some secrets."

Her eyes blinked open and she knuckled away the dampness. She fully intended to pursue that particular secret, but it could wait for another time. "Okay then," she said, drawing back, "what about that thing you do with watches? Stopping them, I mean. How do you do that?"

He just laughed, another secret apparently. And then he began to stroke the hollow of her throat in the most heart-catching way. "Speaking of stopping time, I've got an idea. I know this mountaintop where you can touch the stars."

"The mountain? You want to go there? Now?"

"There, somewhere, *anywhere* . . . all I need is a starry night and a Rain Maiden who dreams about being carried off."

Lord, she thought, it was a dangerous thing falling in love with a man who knew your fantasies. "But we can't, Stephen. There's Em—"

"Em is all right, Lise. She *is* all right, trust me." His blue eyes touched hers, flaring as though with some special knowledge that only he had. "She doesn't need us now. And we do. Need *us*. Come on, Lise, the clock has already started ticking. Let's run away together. Anywhere you want to go, I don't care, but let's not waste another precious second."

She let out the sighing softness that had become her inevitable response to him.

His long fingers swam in her hair, contracting as though he were fighting the need to make love to her right then and there. "I'd better tell them we're leaving," he said, glancing at his watch. "Hey—! *My* watch has stopped." He did a double take and looked up at

Lise, his eyes sparkling with curiosity. "How did you do that?"

Lise smiled and raised on her tiptoes, touching her mouth to his. "My secret," she said as a sweet little shock tingled her lips. "But you might want to check the batteries."

"Batteries?" He laughed through the emotion welling in his voice and glanced up at the sky. "Not a chance, Miss Anderson. This is a sign. This is someone's way of telling us it's going to be all right, that we don't have to rush crazily through life, stealing every moment, counting every second . . . that time will stand still when we're together."

Lise pressed warm against his body, aware of his heartbeat as she searched the night sky with him. She expected a lightning bolt, but all she saw was stars, a rich and endless corridor of stars. There were enough for several lifetimes, and she intended to touch every one of them in one way or another. Because now he was here . . . the hero of her past, the soul mate of her future . . . and anything was possible.

THE EDITOR'S CORNER

What could be more romantic—Valentine's Day and six LOVESWEPT romances all in one glorious month. And I have the great pleasure of writing my first editor's corner. Let me introduce myself: My name is Nita Taublib, and I have worked as an editorial consultant with the Loveswept staff since Loveswept began. As Carolyn is on vacation and Susann is still at home with her darling baby daughter, I have the honor of introducing the fabulous reading treasures we have in store for you. February is a super month for LOVESWEPT!

Deborah Smith's heroes are always fascinating, and in **THE SILVER FOX AND THE RED-HOT DOVE**, LOVESWEPT #450, the mysterious T. S. Audubon is no exception. He is intrigued by the shy Russian woman who accompanies a famous scientist to a party. And he finds himself filled with a desire to help her escape from her keepers! But when Elena Petrovic makes her own desperate escape, she is too terrified to trust him. Could her handsome enigmatic white-haired rescuer be the silver fox of her childhood fantasy, the only man who could set her loose from a hideous captivity, or does he plan to keep her for himself? Mystery and romance are combined in this passionate tale that will move you to tears.

What man could resist having a gorgeous woman as a bodyguard? Well, as Gail Douglas shows in **BANNED IN BOSTON**, LOVESWEPT #451, rugged and powerful Matt Harper never expects a woman to show up when his mother hires a security consultant to protect him after he receives a series of threatening letters. Annie Brentwood is determined to prove that the best protection de-

(continued)

mands brains, not brawn. But she forgets that she must also protect herself from the shameless, arrogant, and oh-so-male Matt, who finds himself intoxicated and intrigued by her feisty spirit. Annie finds it hard to resist a man who promises her the last word and I guarantee you will find this a hard book to put down.

Patt Bucheister's hero in **TROPICAL STORM**, LOVESWEPT #452, will make your temperature rise to sultry heights as he tries to woo Cass Mason. Wyatt Brodie has vowed to take Cass back to Key West for a reconciliation with her desperately ill mother. He challenges her to face her past, promising to help if she'll let him. Can she dare surrender to the hunger he has ignited in her yearning heart? Wyatt has warned her that once he makes love to her, they can never be just friends, that he'll fight to keep her from leaving the island. Can he claim the woman he's branded with the fire of his need? Don't miss this very touching, very emotional story.

From the sunny, sultry South we move to snowy Denver in **FROM THIS DAY FORWARD**, LOVESWEPT #453, by Joan Elliot Pickart. John-Trevor Payton has been assigned to befriend Paisley Kane to discover if sudden wealth and a reunion with the father she's never known will bring her happiness or despair. When Paisley knocks John-Trevor into a snowdrift and falls into his arms, his once firmly frozen plans for eternal bachelorhood begin to melt. Paisley has surrounded herself with a patchwork family of nutty boarders in her Denver house, and John-Trevor envies the pleasure she gets from the people she cares for. But Paisley fears she must choose between a fortune and the man destined to

(continued)

be hers. Don't miss this wonderful romance—a real treat for the senses!

Helen Mittermeyer weaves another fascinating story of two lovers reunited in **THE MASK,** LOVE-SWEPT #455. When Cas Griffith lost his young bride to a plane crash over Nepal he was full of grief and guilt and anger. He believed he'd never again want a woman as he'd desired Margo, but when he comes face-to-face with the exotic, mysterious T'ang Qi in front of a New York art gallery two years later, he feels his body come to life again—and knows he must possess the artist who seems such an unusual combination of East and West. The reborn love discovered through their suddenly intimate embraces stuns them both as they seek to exorcise the ghosts of past heartbreak with a love that knows the true meaning of forever.

Sandra Chastain's stories fairly sizzle with powerful emotion and true love, and for this reason we are thrilled to bring you **DANNY'S GIRL,** LOVE-SWEPT #454. Katherine Sinclair had found it hard to resist the seductive claim Danny Dark's words had made on her heart when she was seventeen. Danny had promised to meet her after graduation, but he never came, leaving her to face a pregnancy alone. She'd given the baby up for adoption, gone to college, ended up mayor of Dark River, and never heard from Danny again . . . until now. Has he somehow discovered that she was raising her son, Mike—their son—now that his adoptive parents had died? Has he returned merely to try to take Mike from her? Danny still makes her burn and ache with a sizzling passion, but once they know the truth about the past, they have to discover if it is love or only memory that has lasted.

(continued)

Katherine longs to show him that they are a family, that the only time she'll ever be happy is in his arms. You won't soon forget this story of two people and their son trying to become a family.

I hope that you enjoy each and every one of these Valentine treats. We've got a great year of reading pleasure in store for you. . . .

Sincerely,

Nita Taublib

Nita Taublib,
Editorial Consultant,
LOVESWEPT
Bantam Books
666 Fifth Avenue
New York, NY 10103

Starting in February . . .

An exciting, unprecedented mass market publishing program designed just for you . . . and the way you buy books!

Over the past few years, the popularity of genre authors has been unprecedented. Their success is no accident, because readers like you demand high levels of quality from your authors and reward them with fierce loyalty.

Now Bantam Books, the foremost English language mass market publisher in the world, takes another giant step in leadership by dedicating the majority of its paperback list to six genre imprints each and every month.

The six imprints that you will see wherever books are sold are:

SPECTRA.

 For five years the premier publisher of science fiction and fantasy. Now Spectra expands to add one title to its list each month, a horror novel.

CRIME LINE.

 The award-winning imprint of crime and mystery fiction. Crime Line will expand to embrace even more areas of contemporary suspense.

DOMAIN.

 An imprint that consolidates Bantam's dominance in the frontier fiction, historical saga, and traditional Western markets.

FALCON.

 High-tech action, suspense, espionage, and adventure novels will all be found in the Falcon imprint, along with Bantam's successful Air & Space and War books.

BANTAM NONFICTION.

 A wide variety of commercial nonfiction, including true crime, health and nutrition, sports, reference books . . . and much more

AND NOW IT IS OUR SPECIAL PLEASURE TO INTRODUCE TO YOU THE SIXTH IMPRINT

FANFARE

FANFARE is the showcase for Bantam's popular women's fiction. With spectacular covers and even more spectacular stories. FANFARE presents three novels each month—ranging from historical to contemporary—all with great human emotion, all with great love stories at their heart, all by the finest authors writing in any genre.

FANFARE LAUNCHES IN FEBRUARY (on sale in early January) WITH THREE BREATHTAK-ING NOVELS . . .

THE WIND DANCER
by Iris Johansen

TEXAS! LUCKY
by Sandra Brown

WAITING WIVES
by Christina Harland

THE WIND DANCER.

From the spellbinding pen of Iris Johansen comes her most lush, dramatic, and emotionally touching romance yet—a magnificent historical about characters whose lives have been touched by the legendary Wind Dancer. A glorious antiquity, the Wind Dancer is a statue of a Pegasus that is encrusted with jewels . . . but whose worth is beyond the value of its precious stones, gold, and artistry. The Wind Dancer's origins are shrouded in the mist of time . . . and only a chosen few can unleash its mysterious powers. But WIND DANCER is, first and foremost, a magnificent love story. Set in Renaissance Italy where intrigues were as intricate as carved cathedral doors and affairs of state were ruled by affairs of the bedchamber. WIND DANCER tells the captivating story of the lovely and indomitable slave Sanchia and the man who bought her on a back street in Florence. Passionate, powerful *condottiere* Lionello Andreas would love Sanchia and endanger her with equal wild abandon as he sought to win back the prized possession of his family, the Wind Dancer.

TEXAS! LUCKY.

Turning her formidable talent for the first time to the creation of a trilogy, Sandra Brown gives readers a family to remember in the Tylers—brothers Lucky and Chase and their "little" sister Sage. In oil-bust country where Texas millionaires are becoming Texas panhandlers, the Tylers are struggling to keep their drilling business from bankruptcy. Each of the TEXAS! novels tells the love story of one member of the family and combines gritty and colorful characters with the fluid and sensual style the author is lauded for!

WAITING WIVES.

By marvelously talented newcomer Christina Harland, WAITING WIVES is the riveting tale of three vastly different women from different countries whose only bond is the fate of their men who are missing in Vietnam. In this unique novel of great human emotion, full of danger, bravery, and romance, Christina Harland brings to the written page what CHINA BEACH and TOUR OF DUTY have brought to television screens. This is a novel of triumph and honor and hope . . . and love.

Rave reviews are pouring in from critics and much-loved authors on FANFARE's novels for February—and for those in months to come. You'll be delighted and enthralled by works by Amanda Quick and Beverly Byrne, Roseanne Bittner and Kay Hooper, Susan Johnson and Nora Roberts . . . to mention only a few of the remarkable authors in the FANFARE imprint.

Special authors. Special covers. And very special stories.

Can you hear the flourish of trumpets now . . . the flourish of trumpets announcing that something special is coming?

FANFARE

Brief excerpts of the launch novels along with praise for them is on the following pages.

New York *Times* bestselling authors Catherine Coulter and Julie Garwood praise the advance copy they read of **WIND DANCER**:

"Iris Johansen is a bestselling author for the best of reasons—she's a wonderful storyteller. Sanchia, Lion, Lorenzo, and Caterina will wrap themselves around your heart and move right in. Enjoy, I did!"
   —Catherine Coulter

"So compelling, so unforgettable a page-turner, this enthralling tale could have been written only by Iris Johansen. I never wanted to leave the world she created with Sanchia and Lion at its center."
   —Julie Garwood

In the following brief excerpt you'll see why *Romantic Times* said this about Iris Johansen and **THE WIND DANCER**:

"The formidable talent of Iris Johansen blazes into incandescent brilliance in this highly original, mesmerizing love story."

We join the story as the evil Carpino, who runs a ring of prostitutes and thieves in Florence, is forcing the young heroine Sanchia to "audition" as a thief for the great *condottiere* Lionello, who waits in the piazza with his friend, Lorenzo, observing at a short distance.

"You're late!" Caprino jerked Sanchia into the shadows of the arcade surrounding the piazza.

"It couldn't be helped," Sanchia said breathlessly. "There was an accident . . . and we didn't get finished until the hour tolled . . . and then I had to wait until Giovanni left to take the—"

Caprino silenced the flow of words with an impatient motion of his hand. "There he is." He nodded across the crowded piazza. "The big man in the wine-colored velvet cape listening to the storyteller."

Sanchia's gaze followed Caprino's to the man standing in front of the platform. He was more than big, he was a giant, she thought gloomily. The careless arrogance in the man's stance bespoke perfect confidence in his ability to deal with any circumstances and, if he caught her, he'd probably use his big strong hands to crush her head like a walnut. Well, she was too tired to worry about that now. It had been over thirty hours since she had slept. Perhaps it was just as well she was almost too exhausted to care what happened to her. Fear must not make her as clumsy as she had been yesterday. She was at least glad the giant appeared able to afford to lose a few ducats. The richness of his clothing indicated he must either be a great lord or a prosperous merchant.

"Go." Caprino gave her a little push out onto the piazza. "Now."

She pulled her shawl over her head to shadow her face and hurried toward the platform where a man was telling a story, accompanying himself on the lyre.

A drop of rain struck her face, and she glanced up at the suddenly dark skies. Not yet, she thought with exasperation. If it started to rain in earnest the people crowding the piazza would run for shelter and she would have to follow the velvet-clad giant until he put himself into a situation that allowed her to make the snatch.

Another drop splashed her hand, and her anxious gaze flew to the giant. His attention was still fixed on the storyteller, but only the saints knew how long he would remain engrossed. This storyteller was not very good. Her pace quickened as she flowed like a shadow into the crowd surrounding the platform.

Garlic, Lion thought, as the odor assaulted his nostrils. Garlic, spoiled fish, and some other stench that smelled even fouler. He glanced around the crowd trying to identify the source of the smell. The people surrounding the platform were the same ones he had studied moments before, trying to search out Caprino's thief. The only new arrival was a thin woman dressed in a shabby gray gown, an equally ragged woolen shawl covering her head.

She moved away from the edge of the crowd and started to hurry across the piazza. The stench faded with her departure and Lion drew a deep breath. *Dio*, luck was with him in this, at least. He was not at all pleased at being forced to stand in the rain waiting for Caprino to produce his master thief.

"It's done," Lorenzo muttered, suddenly at Lion's side. He had been watching from the far side of the crowd. Now he said more loudly, "As sweet a snatch as I've ever seen."

"What?" Frowning, Lion gazed at him. "There was no—" He broke off as he glanced down at his belt. The pouch was gone; only the severed cords remained in his belt. "Sweet Jesus." His gaze flew around the piazza. "Who?"

"The sweet madonna who looked like a beggar maid and smelled like a decaying corpse." Lorenzo nodded toward the arched arcade. "She disappeared behind that column, and I'll wager you'll find Caprino lurking there with her, counting your ducats."

Lion started toward the column. "A woman," he murmured. "I didn't expect a woman. How good is she?"

Lorenzo fell into step with him. "Very good."

Iris Johansen's fabulous romances of characters whose lives are touched by the Wind Dancer go on! STORM WINDS, coming from FANFARE in June 1991, is another historical. REAP THE WIND, a contemporary, will be published by FANFARE in November 1991.

Sandra Brown, whose legion of fans catapulted her last contemporary novel onto the *New York Times* list, has received the highest praise in advance reviews of **TEXAS! LUCKY**. *Rave Reviews* said, "Romance fans will relish all of Ms. Brown's provocative sensuality along with a fast-paced plotline that springs one surprise after another. Another feast for the senses from one of the world's hottest pens."

Indeed Sandra's pen is "hot"—especially so in her incredible **TEXAS!** trilogy. We're going to peek in on an early episode in which Lucky has been hurt in a brawl in a bar where he was warding off the attentions of two town bullies toward a redhead he hadn't met, but wanted to get to know very well.

This woman was going to be an exciting challenge, something rare that didn't come along every day. Hell, he'd never had anybody exactly like her.

"What's your name?"

She raised deep forest-green eyes to his. "D-D Dovey."

" 'D-D Dovey'?"

"That's right," she snapped defensively. "What's wrong with it?"

"Nothing. I just hadn't noticed your stuttering before. Or has the sight of my bare chest made you develop a speech impediment?"

"Hardly. Mr.—?"

"Lucky."

"Mr. Lucky?"

"No, I'm Lucky."

"Why is that?"

"I mean my name is Lucky. Lucky Tyler."

"Oh. Well. I assure you the sight of your bare chest leaves me cold, Mr. Tyler."

He didn't believe her and the smile that tilted up one corner of his mouth said so. "Call me Lucky."

She reached for the bottle of whiskey on the nightstand and raised it in salute. "Well, Lucky, your luck just ran out."

"Huh?"

"Hold your breath." Before he could draw a sufficient one, she tipped the bottle and drizzled the liquor over the cut.

He blasted the four walls with words unfit to be spoken aloud, much less shouted. "Oh hell, oh—"

"Your language isn't becoming to a gentleman, Mr. Tyler."

"I'm gonna murder you. Stop pouring that stuff— Agh!"

"You're acting like a big baby."

"What the hell are you trying to do, scald me?"

"Kill the germs."

"Damn! It's killing *me*. Do something. Blow on it."

"That only causes germs to spread."

"Blow on it!"

She bent her head over his middle and blew gently along the cut. Her breath fanned his skin and cooled the stinging whiskey in the open wound. Droplets of it had collected in the satiny stripe of hair beneath his navel. Rivulets trickled beneath the waistband of his jeans. She blotted at them with her fingertips, then, without thinking, licked the liquor off her own skin. When she realized what she'd done, she sprang upright. "Better now?" she asked huskily.

When Lucky's blue eyes connected with hers, it was like completing an electric circuit. The atmosphere crackled. Matching her husky tone of voice, he said, "Yeah, much better. . . . Thanks," he mumbled. Her hand felt so comforting and cool, the way his mother's always had whenever he was sick with fever. He captured Dovey's hand with his and pressed it against his hot cheek.

She withdrew it and, in a schoolmarm's voice, said, "You can stay only until the swelling goes down."

"I don't think I'll be going anywhere a-tall tonight," he said. "I feel like hell. This is all I want to do. Lie here. Real still and quiet."

Through a mist of pain, he watched her remove her jacket and drape it over the back of a chair. Just as he'd thought—quite a looker was Dovey. But that wasn't all. She looked like a woman who knew her own mind and wasn't afraid to speak it. Levelheaded.

So what the hell had she been doing in that bar? He drifted off while puzzling through the question.

Now on sale in DOUBLEDAY hardcover is the next in Sandra's fantastic trilogy, TEXAS! CHASE, about which *Rendezvous* has said: ". . . it's the story of a love that is deeper than the oceans, and more lasting than the land itself. Lucky's story was fantastic; Chase's story is more so." FANFARE's paperback of TEXAS! CHASE will go on sale August 1991.

Rather than excerpt from the extraordinary novel **WAITING WIVES**, which focuses on three magnificent women, we will describe the book in some detail. The three heroines whom you'll love and root for give added definition to the words growth and courage . . . and love.

ABBRA is talented and sheltered, a raven-haired beauty who was just eighteen when she fell rapturously in love with handsome Army captain Lewis Ellis. Immediately after their marriage he leaves for Vietnam. Passionately devoted to Lewis, she lives for his return—until she's told he's dead. Then her despair turns to torment as she falls hopelessly in love with Lewis's irresistible brother. . . .

SERENA never regrets her wildly impulsive marriage to seductive Kyle Anderson. But she does regret her life of unabashed decadence and uninhibited pleasure—especially when she discovers a dirty, bug-infested orphanage in Saigon . . . and Kyle's illegitimate child.

GABRIELLE is the daughter of a French father and a Vietnamese mother. A flame-haired singer with urchin appeal and a sultry voice, she is destined for stardom. But she gives her heart—and a great part of her future—to a handsome Aussie war correspondent. Gavin is determined to record the "real" events of the Vietnam war . . . but his search for truth leads him straight into the hands of the Viet Cong and North Vietnamese, who have no intention of letting him report anything until they've won the war.

Christina Harland is an author we believe in. Her story is one that made all of us who work on FANFARE cry, laugh, and turn pages like mad. We predict that WAITING WIVES will fascinate and enthrall you . . . and that you will say with us, "it is a novel whose time has come."

We hope you will greet FANFARE next month with jubilation! It is an imprint we believe you will delight in month after month, year after year to come.

THE "VIVE LA ROMANCE" SWEEPSTAKES

Don't miss your chance to speak to your favorite Loveswept authors on the LOVESWEPT LINE 1-900-896-2505*

You may win a glorious week for two in the world's most romantic city, Paris, France by entering the "Vive La Romance" sweepstakes when you call. With travel arrangements made by Reliable Travel, you and that special someone will fly American Airlines to Paris, where you'll be guests at the famous Lancaster Hotel. Why not call right now? Your own Loveswept fantasy could come true!

Official Rules:

1. **No Purchase Is Necessary.** Enter by calling 1-900-896-2505 and following the directions for entry. The phone call will cost $.95 per minute and the average time necessary to enter the sweepstakes will be two minutes or less with either a touch tone or a rotary phone, when you choose to enter at the beginning of the call. Or you can enter by handprinting your name, address and telephone number on a plain 3" x 5" card and sending it to:

> **VIVE LA ROMANCE SWEEPSTAKES**
> **Department CK**
> **BANTAM BOOKS**
> **666 Fifth Avenue**
> **New York, New York 10103**

Copies of the Official Rules can be obtained by sending a request along with a self-addressed stamped envelope to: Vive La Romance Sweepstakes, Bantam Books, Department CK-2, 666 Fifth Avenue, New York, New York 10103. Residents of Washington and Vermont need not include return postage. Requests must be received by November 30, 1990.

*Callers must be 18 or older. Each call costs 95¢ per minute. See official rules for details.

Loveswept ®